Creative Writing Heals
Volume 4

A new collection from Converge writers
at York St John University 2021

Creative Writing Heals: Volume 4
First published in 2022
by Writing Tree Press

All rights reserved. No part of this publication may be reproduced, stored in a database or retrieval system, or transmitted, in any form or by any means, without the prior permission in writing of the publisher, nor be otherwise circulated in any form or binding or cover other than that in which it is published and without a similar condition including this condition being imposed on the subsequent purchaser.

© 2022 respective authors
Cover art © 2022 by Sylkie de Waard

The moral rights of the authors have been asserted.
All characters and events in this publication, other than those clearly in the public domain, are fictitious, and any resemblance to any real person, living or dead, is purely coincidental and not intended by the authors.

The right of Helen Kenwright to be identified as the editor of this work has been asserted by her in accordance with Section 77 of the Copyright, Designs and Patents Act 1988

For information contact:
Writing Tree Press, Unit 10773, PO Box 4336
Manchester, M61 0BW
www.writingtree.co.uk

Contents

Foreword 3

Beautiful Human by Llykaell Dert-Ethrae 5

Why me... why not? by Richard Hall 7

Poems by Holly 17

Charlotte by Christina O'Reilly 19

A Physical Presence by Zofia Ellis 33

Meeting Up by Keith Myers 48

Church of the Green Cross by Michael Fairclough . 50

Instructions on Making Quilts...the English Method

by Stuart Hillard 62

Blind Bride by Mary C Palmer 73

Pennsylvania Hexes by Joe Murray-Smith 81

The Reclaimed by Minnie Lansell 89

The Honour of a Thief by Junior Mark Cryle 105

We Are The Gordons!

by Caroline Stockwell-Brown 111

Village Lives by Catherine Dean 121

Job Satisfaction by Karen 135

Oxtinction: Consequences of the Ungrateful
Popullution by TNX 141

This is Our Space by Lucy Waters 142
I'd Like to Play Guitar and other poems
by Mary C Palmer 153
The Last Great Bin Find by Kevin Keld..................158
Maeve Quinn by Esther Clare Griffiths 167
The Four Horsemen on the Bus by Milly Watson ..177
This is Where the Magic Happens
By Helen Kenwright 187
The Diaries of Pandemic Objects
by Abbie-Rose Reddington....................................188
A Legacy of Celestials and Amphibians
by Llykaell Dert-Ethrae 192
Mindful Guidance By Christina O'Reilly.................196
Some Things Never Change
by Junior Mark Cryle...197
The Nature of Flame by Ross 204
Tansy by William Davidson 207
The Miracle of Our Hands by Charley Perryn........210
About Our Authors..213
Acknowledgements 221
About Converge..223
About the Writing Tree..225

Foreword

This year's collection of writing features work by writers I have never met in person; some of whom I haven't seen at all, not even as a name in a Zoom chat or a face in a neat video rectangle. In the 2020-21 academic year we were rudely excluded from campus thanks to the ongoing pandemic.

But Converge, as always, refused to be postponed, and looked to explore new ways of learning together. We continued the Zoom sessions we'd switched to during the first lockdown with fresh confidence and ingenuity. More and more students found their way to our virtual classrooms. We were able to offer students an expanded provision we'd never offered before.

We met new students, too, some of whom would not have been able to join our campus classes even if we hadn't been locked down. We provided correspondence courses for those who preferred to learn offline, and soon came eagerly to anticipate the letters and work that arrived from students in old fashioned envelopes.

This worked so well that we're keeping it. When we returned to campus in the Autumn we launched Converge Connected so that we can offer online and postal versions alongside our traditional classes for the foreseeable future.

Throughout this adventure our students have continued to excel, as you'll see in the stories and poems which follow. Whether you like a romantic heist, a zombie horror story or a reflection on village life, it's all here, and much, much more.

So get yourself a cuppa, curl up in your favourite spot and enjoy.

Helen Kenwright
February 2022

Beautiful Human

by Llykaell Dert-Ethrae

Absolute power in a powerless form.
So fragile
Mortal
A broken twig on a winding river
Where nothing exists, where everything thrives.
Seeking command over all things,
Seeing only then they had the strength of gods
While bearing nothing at all.
This empty world -
This mortal shell,
With muscles coiled
Sweat-laden brows
And gritted teeth
It stands against all things.
Even devoid of omniscience
Magick
And all manner of control
They fight with abandon
Unceasing
Unyielding
Indomitable.
It is here gods are surpassed
As was their intent
For children become what their parents could not.
Perfection is weakness
It is powerless.
For absolute authority is hollow

And only consumes itself.
Along the waves of the sea
Hurtled helplessly against its currents
There it is we find our strength.
The truest power comes from nothing
And from within,
To be wielded without intent to dominate
As the defender of all things.
There is no great tribulation
That through such adversity
It will fail to surmount.
It will match every step
Now and forever
Without the need for anything other than itself
For it ever ascends -
The Lone Conqueror.
From nothing is everything
And from everything there is nothing
For the Love we hold
Is a contradiction
And the seed from which
The blossom of omnipotence is born.

To hold nothing in the palm of your hand
Is to have everything in all creation.

Why me ...why not?

by Richard Hall

1959 was not the most memorable year for most people. However, it was in this year that Fidel Castro came to power and NASA announced its selection of seven military pilots that would become the first US astronauts.

But there was a bigger event looming in June of that year. Yours truly made his appearance, with a big Hiya! And how you doing! Which wasn't expected or planned.

So June the 17th 1959 was a day of joy and happiness, if no doubt with a little apprehension. Back in the late 50s and early 60s it wasn't thought or seen as socially acceptable to be having children so late in life as it is currently.

My mum was 46 years old and my father was 51 years old, and no doubt friends and colleagues of theirs were discussing and deliberating the positives and negatives of my arrival at this late stage in my parents' lives.

Mum and Dad, who were neither particularly religious, nor considered themselves that old, and were still very active, could only see the positives in having a child late in life and felt fortunate and quite blessed. My father had ran away from his family at the age of 14, a true travelling family that, may I add, never actually travelled anywhere! They resided in the local woods, and provided pit ponies for the local mines in County Durham for the previous 30 years in order to make a living.

I guess he could already see the future wasn't in coal mines, long before Maggie came along and started closing them all. So off he trotted aged 14 to the army recruiting centre, lied about his age and joined the Army. (You had to be 16.) There he went on to spend the next 34 years and became a commissioned officer, serving through the Second World War, and been part of the Dunkirk landings, something he never really spoke about.

It was while in the army that he met my mum, just before the start of the Second World War, while she was working in the Home office. I mention this because by the time I arrived, both my parents were retired and living a very comfortable life on their army pensions.

I feel it necessary to give you a brief history and insight with regards my parents, because this was going lead to a very different childhood and upbringing for yours truly, although obliviously I didn't realise this at the time.

My childhood school holidays were spent fly fishing for salmon and trout just over the Scottish border, where my parents owned a small cottage at the side of the river Esk. By nine years old I could fly fish as good as any grown-up.

And this, my friends, is what led to my first recommendation for the need for therapy....Supposedly?

It was the last day at primary school before we broke up for the eagerly awaited 6 week summer holidays, and the playground chatter was all about the "Mouse" which apparently was the scariest roller coaster ride in Europe in 1969. It was situated at Blackpool pleasure beach and, according to playground rumour, very few kids would actually dare to ride it.

This was never going to be a problem for me: my school holiday plans didn't include visiting Blackpool or such like coastal resorts. Instead, I was off to Donegal in Ireland for two weeks fly fishing with my parents and the odd day at a rural beach, with any luck.

That was to be followed by a week in Aberdeenshire fishing a river called the Dee. According to my father this was one of the finest salmon fishing rivers in Europe, with a succession of salmon pools with fast-flowing crystal clear water that every serious fly fisherman must fish. Which I guess made sense as we were driving to Ireland and going over on the ferry, from Stranraer to Larne, which was something I was quite excited by. And then returning in two weeks to Stranraer in Scotland via the ferry. Two for one deal for me, so not all bad.

We had a glorious two weeks in Donegal, great sunshine, great fishing and I got to visit some of Donegal's finest beaches. With my dinghy, snorkel and flippers, I also came across my first Jellyfish - not something I would recommend or make a habit of in the future, but that's another story for another time.

We arrived at our bed and breakfast in Ballater in the late afternoon, after leaving the ferry terminal in Stranraer and what seemed like a never-ending drive to get there. So it was an early dinner and early bed for me, as we had an 06.00 start in the morning. Mum wasn't coming; she was off exploring the Balmoral area and castle, no doubt hoping to bump into Lizzy. So it was just Dad and I fishing for the next few days.

We arrived bright and early at the old Balmoral bridge, dropping mum off and parking the car. Then we got our fishing tackle together for the day, including lunch, coffee and fizzy drinks, as we had a mile and a half to hike to get to the pools we were allowed to fish, so my father informed me. Along the route, I was informed how great this river was for salmon fishing, including how it stretches for ninety miles flowing through the Cairngorms until it reaches the North Sea at Aberdeen.

We finally arrived at our destination after some 40 minutes of walking through some really stunning countryside. Even at nine years old I could really appreciate the scenic grandeur. Once again I was given the importance of the rules. (Each time you cast you must take a step down the pool, and I wasn't allowed to cross the river or go on the opposite bank).

I was starting at the first of the nine pools we were to fish that day and my father was starting at the pool below me. I had fished several pools all morning, not had a bite, and, if I'm honest, I was having some serious doubts about how great this river was for salmon fishing. Then I noticed several figures high up across river bank at the far side, watching me quite intently, probably four to five hundred yards away. Until that moment I hadn't seen a soul for hours.

Probably some fifty minutes later, I heard some barking behind me along the riverbank. I turned to see two men with a couple of Black Labradors heading down the bank towards me. One looked like Sherlock Holmes, dressed in a tweed suit, plus fours and deerstalker, the other chap was clearly a water bailiff or ghillie dressed in the standard waxed coat, cords, and heavyset brogues on his feet, carrying a Browning shotgun. Panic immediately set in: these guys were the equivalent of London's flying squad (The Sweeney) in the world of river and salmon fishing law, and I had no paperwork with me or proof I was entitled to fish here. My father had it with him, and was probably several hundred yards down the river, well out of sight at the time.

Poaching salmon was big business in Scotland and many people made a good living from it, but it was a cat and mouse game played by those who poached and the water bailiffs; sometimes it was very confrontational and could occasionally end in violence. Hence most water bailiffs tended to carry shotguns as part of their everyday work tools, but it was quite intimidating for a nine-year-old, to say the least.

They finally approached the edge of the river and asked me if I could wade out, as they would like a word with me. I was shaking more than my mum's old twin tub washer did when it was on a fast spin. After asking my name and who I was with, I started giving them said details. Looking back, it always amazed me how they managed to understand me, given my stuttering and shaking while trying to speak. Was this my first sign of suffering from anxiety?

They thanked me for my help and proceeded to walk off back the way they had come, which was surprising, as I expected them to continue downstream, towards where my father was and check our paperwork and my details with Dad.

I returned to my fishing, after considering going to find my father and inform him of my visit from the water police, but I guessed he would be coming to find me shortly as it was well past lunchtime. Some fifty minutes had passed when I heard the sound of a clanky old diesel Land Rover coming bumbling along the riverbank, which was strange and worrying at the same time, as no vehicles were allowed on this area of land and I hadn't seen any way you could get one down here. I hadn't noticed any gates or openings while walking to our fishing area.

The long-wheelbase standard green Land Rover pulled up opposite me on the edge of the bank, and the same two chaps with the same two black labs got out followed by another chap and older woman. I thought I was in some serious trouble now, as the new two people were probably the landowners, and they obviously hadn't believed one word I had said previously.

So once again I waded out of the river, the labs came bounding up like they were my best friends, and the group of four approached me. It was the lady who spoke first this time and asked me how old I was and how long I had been fly fishing. She had that typical reassuring and friendly grandma voice.

I said I was soon to be ten and had been fly fishing for the last three year; the lady commented how she had never seen anyone of my age cast out so accurately and so far, and how wonderful it was to see, to which I commented that my father had taught me how to fly fish, and I had spent most of my school holidays fishing. At which point my father came round the curve of the river, some two hundred yards away. I guess he'd heard the clanky old diesel Land Rover rock up and had come to see what was going on.

The new chap, who hadn't spoken to me at all, started off heading towards my father. This wasn't looking good at all in my mind. The lady was still speaking to me, but even to this day I can't remember what she said - or probably I didn't even hear her, I was so focused on my dad approaching and this stranger shooting off to intercept him.

Finally, my dad arrived after chatting to the stranger, and then bowed and took his fishing cap off. He addressed the lady in some formal way that I had never heard before, but it all sounded polite and friendly, yet no one had asked my dad for the documents and licenses to fish here, so I wandered off a few yards playing with the two black labs, while a short conversation was held, probably about two minutes, and the group of four headed back to their old Land Rover and Dad came over and said time for lunch.

The six weeks school summer holidays always

seemed to fly by at that time in my life. So first day back at school in my final year and it was in the days of the eleven plus which decided if you went to grammar school or a secondary modern. Mr Shann, our form teacher for our final year at primary school, was also our English teacher. So it was no surprise in our English lesson on our first day back we had to write about what we did and where we went during the summer holidays, which I duly did, along with every other kid in the class.

The dreaded parents evening arrived some months later, I'm sure you all remember it: it was the one where you got grounded for two weeks or rewarded with lots of praise and could get away with murder for a few days, depending on how your teacher reported to your parents on how well you were doing and how well behaved you were in class or not as the case might be.

My mum sat there listening to Mr Shann who in all fairness was giving me a pretty good report on the year. But he concluded by telling my mum that for all that, educationally-wise, I was making great progress and he didn't see any reason why I wouldn't pass my eleven plus, she may like to consider taking me to see a child psychologist.....What!!!!

My mum apparently sat there with a mouth open and totally lost for words, stunned at this revelation. Having gathered herself together, she finally asked him on what grounds and reasons did he think this course of action was necessary? Mr Shann went on to explain that in his humble opinion he thought yours truly had a problem telling the difference between reality and fiction, be it through reading or watching television was his suggestions. Yes, I did read a lot as a kid and still do to this day, television probably less than the average kid then and person these days. His evidence and data to back up this recommendation were based on my writing over the last three years in English classes, where he informed my mum that I wrote stories as if I was an adult, as in driving cars, riding motorcycles, fishing, shooting, travelling to Norway to salmon fish, training German pointer gun dogs to work in the field, but apparently, the final straw was my last writing submission of what I did in the last school holidays. Which he produced like Rumpole of the Bailey to show my mum, and which she read through.

After a short pause, Mr Shann said, "I'm sure that you can understand my concerns Mrs Hall."

To which my mum replied, "And they are...?"

"Well for starters, I would think meeting the Queen Mum and receiving praise from her Royal Highness on his ability to fly fish and having a chat with his dad, and with such great detail, would give cause for concern? And let's not forget he claims to have been driving your husband's Volvo144 for the last year and being allowed to do so by himself, be it across farmland and country tracks."

My mum stood up and no doubt got great pleasure and no doubt some relief from reassuring Mr Shann, that everything he had pointed out to her that I had written was, in fact, true and correct, and maybe he should stick to teaching English rather than an amateur child psychologist.

For the record, for all Mr Shann has no doubt long passed away, I salute you Sir. I did pass my eleven plus and attend grammar school, but more than that I got a Raleigh Chopper bike for doing so. I can't help feeling that Mr Shann's recommendation of my need for a child psychologist may have contributed to the over-the-top reward!

Poems
by Holly

Recovery

"Arts lift wellbeing and aids recovery," she said.
as a brush coated my memories with brightness,
building a facade upon the negativity
of the memories hidden within.
I could paint myself a new future,
I couldn't do anything about the past.
And yet I was here,
willingly,
searching for some type of positivity.
Mixing colours chaotically with my hands
observing myself
how my body functioned
grounding myself in feelings
an anxiety inducing progress.

Shadow of a friend

Wind grasping the flag, leaving it shaking
breeze drifting on.
I was the only person alone.
Leant against the building
the sun stared down
leaving a shadow in front of me
my only companion.
And we still couldn't look eye to eye.

Daffodils

She grew
without worry
into a world so uncertain
she was so unprepared
unaware
and somehow
she brought hope

Pens

Without any pens
It is difficult to write
A clever haiku

Charlotte

by Christina O'Reilly

Introduction

She was standing in the window where she should have been waiting for the signal; she was holding the blue hanky in her hand that she would have signalled back with, but she'd cancelled that arrangement via telegram. Bertie would be getting a nasty surprise this morning. Today was her graduation day, today was the start of her new life, but not the one she'd expected. Her brother was still home, he had no idea of what was going on, as he sat in his big blue bat-winged chair which he'd taken over from her father, his head in the newspapers. He thinks she doesn't know but she does, he's in for a big shock tonight, she could have been in for a bigger one if she hadn't been out two weeks ago Wednesday. She would still be thinking she was going to elope with Bertie. What a life would she have had, if she hadn't found out what her brother Samuel, Bertie and the others were up to.

This should have crushed her, changed her forever. It had in a way; she was stronger than all of them knew, thanks to her father Henry Chambers and her new friends. At least, she hoped they were her friends. She'd even surprised herself. Thank God Bertie had met her for lunch at the little inn by the river; Charlotte had had to wait for her carriage. That's when she'd seen them meet.

This is Charlotte's story.

Chapter 1
Finding out

Bertie had been flustered, fidgeting all the time, looking over her shoulder, hardly touching his meal. She'd asked if he was feeling unwell but he'd denied it, then suddenly ended their lunch, saying she must leave ahead of him as he wanted to keep their secret safe... their plans had been in place for quite some time, so why the panic?

When she'd paid the bill, Billy the innkeeper looked at Bertie with contempt then turned away. Bertie never noticed; he was too busy preening.

As she was getting ready to leave, Bertie suddenly grabbed Charlotte's hand, asking if she'd sorted everything out, if the property was in joint names, was the wedding licence ready? Funny, she thought he wasn't interested in any of that, but it hadn't seemed right. She'd felt unnerved by it, he'd never rushed her before.

Billy had tucked her away in a corner booth hidden away from the dining hall as there were a number of carriages disembarking people; it was a stopover for travellers. He'd said it wouldn't be long. It was a quiet nook, Billy had said he could keep an eye on her too. She'd smiled.

She was sitting sipping a tisane of lemon, honey

and herbs when she'd heard him. She didn't see him, just the shadow of him rushing by.

"Innkeep!" he'd shouted, "Your best red wine, and keep it coming!"

She spotted her brother Samuel. He seemed so happy; she'd not seen that in him in quite a while, but Billy stood in the entrance flapping his bar cloth behind his back as if to say stay where you are. She stayed sitting as he guided her brother and another guest to their seats.

She peeped between the latticework dividing her from the dining area and, to her surprise, Bertie stood up. As Samuel sat down, so did the other person - it was her father's old partner, Mr Bradly. They leaned into each other conspiratorially, and she was shocked, shaking, sick, flushed; she didn't understand, they didn't know each other - but clearly they did.

"Is our regular room ready?" she heard Samuel ask.

"Yes," said Billy. "Dinner will be served in about twenty-five minutes. Your room hasn't been touched since you met last. You have time to relax with your drinks."

Billy came and got her. He took her through a snicket at the end of the bench she was sitting on. Pushing her through the servant's stairwell to the floor above, saying, "I know this is happening so very fast miss, but, you need to know what's going on, you must see the documents that they have on you, you must protect yourself..." They went into a room which had been laid out as an office, where Billy showed her the documents. Charlotte was the subject of them; she read and took what she could, but it was so rushed, her feet didn't touch the ground. Billy had Charlotte's arm; they heard footsteps on the stairs below; he pushed her through a small door down another set of stairs and out by the kitchen. There, waiting for Charlotte, was her carriage.

Charlotte needed to take action quickly but who to trust? Who? Charlotte scanned the documents through tears but she could see that all the documents had been signed by the people her father had trusted.

The saddest thing was knowing her brother was behind all of this.

Chapter 2
Henry and Samuel

How sad.... All over the death of Henry, her sweet father, how he must be withering in his grave.

When Henry had died, he'd made Charlotte the sole heir to his fortune. She knew something was going to happen as Henry had said "Stay strong," and "I have true faith in all your abilities." He'd been training her in a funny way: taking her to the office, introducing her to all the staff, giving her vast quantities of work under the pretext that he was swamped and needed her support. God bless you, Father.

Henry had left Samuel with what Samuel called a 'meagre inheritance', which did not sit well with him at all. "Meagre" it was not. Samuel had been a bitter disappointment to Henry: he'd failed at school, he'd failed at Henry's office, he'd been caught with his hand in the petty cash, and he'd failed at starting up his own business, he'd had to be bailed out time and time again.

Samuel's first tactic was to say Henry was mad and try to get his will overturned. Henry had had the foresight to know that Samuel would try this, so he'd had his doctor, bank manager and solicitor be witnesses to the will. He also, unbeknownst to anyone, had Mr May, a specialist in London, give him a complete mental and physical overhaul and pronounce him sound in all areas. When Mr May, a very prominent and respected gentleman in his field, had turned up at court, Samuel had had to give up.

He then tried to force Charlotte's hand by trying to get the bank to agree to joint signatures on accounts, saying that Charlotte was not capable of running their father's legacy. Again, Henry had foreseen this, and in his will he'd added that he had trained her for business, that she had passed all her accounting exams taken with the First Ladies University. He had stated that only his beloved daughter Charlotte could withdraw all funds from accounts, buy and sell any of his stocks, run his company, and also that all the properties were to be her responsibility too. (So that's what Henry was up to with Miss Lace...) A tutor at the university would come twice over a ten day period, getting her to fill in forms, doing what she'd thought were test papers to prepare her for the real thing (sneaky). Henry worked her hard; she'd almost thrown everything in but, looking at her father, she could see things weren't right and now she knew why.

Chapter 3

What to do - who could she trust

The next day she was a little on edge (not surprising). Samuel was sitting in his chair and all she felt was contempt for him. She put her coat on, saw him peek over his paper.

"Going out?" he said.

"Yes," was all she replied. She had no doubt that he knew she wasn't seeing Bertie. He asked if she wanted company but she said, "No. I'm going to the First Ladies University."

He snorted. She gave him a stern look and turned away, but not before she saw his surprise at her tone.

She wasn't lying, she was on the way to the University to see Miss Lace, she was the only person who had known what was happening at home. But would she help her? All Charlotte could do was ask.

To her surprise, Miss Lace had been expecting her.

Miss Lace told Charlotte not to take her coat off, but to go to Little Vale Lane. A few turnings down on her right there was a Tea Room called 'Milady'. The owner was a good friend of hers called Sally; it was a Ladies Tea Room, and she could meet her there. She wanted to see if anyone was following her. She could take her time to visit the emporium and a couple of smaller stores on the way without looking over her shoulder. She wouldn't be far behind. If anyone asked, she would talk about the Graduation ceremony on Friday, making sure she was sounding gracious and praising her father's encouragement and belief in her.

She asked friends if they would like to come as her father was gone and she had no one to stand for her.

She told Miss Lace everything when she arrived, and Miss Lace said she had been 'thinking on her feet', 'outstanding' and 'brilliant'. Charlotte smiled to herself. Firstly, they moved to a room upstairs in the little tea shop - no one else would be allowed upstairs for the duration of the meeting. She was surprised to see two gentlemen sitting awaiting them when they arrived. It turned out that Miss Lace was ahead of her game. One of the gentlemen was a Pinkerton Marshall, Davy Bridge, and the other was a solicitor called Mr Whitby from Hayfield, a small town about six miles away. He said he often worked with the Pinkerton Agency. She was to find out the address of the Agency for herself, send a telegram and wait for a reply to check they were who they say they were.

She called on some of her father's friends on the way home, inviting those she thought would stand for her if required. Most seemed happy to see she was in good health.

Charlotte sent a telegram to Pinkerton Agency, awaiting the reply which she'd get in a few hours if all was well. She sent invites to all relevant parties.

Charlotte arranged a lunch at Milady tea rooms and the dinner would be at the little inn on the river (funnily enough it was actually called 'The Little Inn on the River'). She'd asked Miss Lace to stay with her as a companion, really another form of protection for Charlotte.

When her brother returned home, she told him that Mr Bridge was now head of security in the house and offices. Two of his officers would be placed at the office day and night. He was not happy, but held on to his temper as Davy was next to her. She felt everything else could wait until after her Graduation. She thought she'd treat herself to two new outfits; Mr Whitby was to draw up all relevant documents ready for signing. She'd also sent a telegram requesting Mr May, the consultant from London, to come tomorrow and not to discuss it with anyone.

Mr May had turned up with his daughter, under the guise of them being on holiday for a few days; he had said he was just checking in to see how they were doing. Samuel left, saying he wanted air and mumbling something about Mr May being an affront to him. Charlotte said she was sad about that as she'd asked them to stay for her Graduation and Dinner at her house. "How dare you," he said, "this is my house" then realised what he said and coughed as Davy stepped out into the hall. Charlotte just smiled at him; he squinted at her and slammed the front door. She told Mr May everything. He told her that Henry had said that if Charlotte need his assistance, he would come to her aid.

Chapter 4
Graduation day

When Charlotte thought she was to marry Bertie, which had been arranged for tomorrow, Charlotte had hidden papers, money etc.... in the attic space she'd found when her foot caught the corner of a panel. She only went to the attic when everybody was out; she'd even made her own dust (a little dry, fine earth and talc) to cover up when she's been up in there. No one, absolutely no one, knew it was there. Today could go horribly wrong and she may need it. She shivered.

As the day progressed, something wonderful happened. She started to receive gifts; flowers with lots of lovely notes of support from family and friends. It made her heart ache with happiness at their kindness. She'd had nothing from her brother. She was wearing her new pale blue suit and the Graduation had gone off without a hitch. To her surprise everyone had clapped and cheered when her name had been called out. A light lunch had been arranged for all the graduates and families at Milady tea rooms. Her brother had pretended to shake her hand and leaning in whispered, "Stop spending all my money." She'd just smiled at him, the same big grin she had before. He had tutted, hissed and turned away, returning to his cohorts in the corner. Everyone seemed to enjoy it, except Samuel of course.

Chapter 5
The Dinner

The Dinner was due to start at 7:30pm, roast chicken with all the trimmings, six assorted vegetables, meat juices and various puddings. Charlotte had asked Samuel to choose the wine stating that she was sure he knew the best red and white of the house and "Keep it coming," she laughed. He looked at her with a quizzical stare but said nothing he hadn't known she was there that day. Sixteen days ago it felt longer.

Charlotte was dressed in a rather lovely amethyst pearl and crystal beaded dress, beautiful. She felt she could conquer the world - and then she felt really ill for what was to come.

Everything was in place. She had arrived ahead of time to check. Billy and his wife Mabel had outdone themselves: the room was wonderful and just for her they had shut the inn for the night.

As friends and family started to arrive, Billy got the band to play. It was all very jolly and lively, but what no one noticed was Davy, Mr Whitby and Mr May quietly taking people up to the room her brother was using (why hadn't he moved it? She'd never know). Charlotte thought they would have to follow this group until they found it again but, that's how confident Samuel was. It just made things easier for her.

The evening was full of laughter and joy. People praised Mable's food and once everyone had had their fill, the tables were moved to the side so the dancing could begin. After the first dance had finished, Samuel grabbed her arm and tried to pull her towards the stairs, but thank goodness someone stepped in-between them. Samuel stopped. He turned bright red. Charlotte knew she had to start her speech. Her brother was beyond angry. His friends were trying to hold him back.

She clapped her hands, the band stopped, everyone turned, a small space was made, Billy put a box down for her to stand on - and so she began:

"I wish to thank you all for coming, and I know

my father would too. A toast to Henry Chambers, a wonderful father and sorely missed." Henry's name rang out in the room. She noticed that Samuel was turning an odder colour with rage.

Now for the first shot at her brother. "Some of you will know that I had quietly made a friendship with Bertie Wimpole; you may also have noticed he's not here. Early this morning I sent him the following telegraph:

Bertie FRIENDSHIP over (stop) You lied saying you didn't know my brother or anyone related to me which was a falsehood (stop) I must now concentrate on the family business (Stop) A member from the Pinkerton Agency will be visiting you to confirm your relationship with Samuel (stop)

She breathed and said, "I now understand that Bertie has left town with the Pinkertons on his trail."

There were a few gasps. Charlotte continued, "Also, today I sent letters to Messrs Pemberley, Lessor, and Markham offices stating that I would no longer be using their services as they have been colluding against me with my brother Samuel, to overturn my father's will. Once married they intended to try and have Bertie have me committed just to get his hands on my family's wealth. This has now been confirmed by the Pinkerton Agency and many here tonight will have seen with their own eyes what my brother has been planning."

More and more gasps went around the room. People started turning to look at Samuel and his cohorts, some of his group were running for the door, others were pushing towards Charlotte. Her brother shouted "Grab her! Grab her!" "Don't let her get away!" Someone tugged her from behind and Charlotte started to fall - it was Henry's ex-partner shouting, "Now you can see how mad she is!" There was a clang and Mr Bradly was out cold on the floor. Mabel had hit him from behind.

Samuel got to her as she hit the floor, dragging her by her hair, kicking her, shouting, "Shut up you filthy liar!"

He had a knife in his hand, swinging it towards her, but stopped when she screamed, "You'll lose everything if this madness continues!"

"I've lost everything anyway," he said.

Charlotte pulled herself to her feet, Mr Bridge had his gun in his hand, Mr May was dealing with a few women who had fainted. Charlotte wanted it to stop. "This is Mr Whitby," she shouted. "He has some documents for you to sign. Your allowance will continue if you agree to see someone at Mr May's clinic in London." She could hear a scuffle still going on outside. "Once you've done that, you'll leave England never to return." She sighed. "It's the only way to know I'll be safe." Charlotte took a deep breath. "Otherwise Mr Bridge will arrest you and everyone involved. It's up to you, a carriage is waiting outside for you and Mr May but you have to sign first. Make your choice now," she said in a voice nobody recognised.

Samuel dropped the knife. No-one had noticed it had blood on it. Samuel walked towards Mr Whitby; Billy and Mr Bridges stood in front of Charlotte. Samuel sighed, "I really loved you once." Then he spat at Charlotte's feet and turned to leave. To everyone's surprise, Charlotte crumpled to the floor holding her side. There was pandemonium. The last thing she heard was Samuel saying, "Die will you! Then I'll get everything!"

There was laughter. Then blackness.

Chapter 6
Hope

Luckily it wasn't too deep a cut, so Charlotte was stitched up and sent home. She was fussed over by all her friends for a week, and then wanted to get on with things. She had her father's butler clear out her brother's belongings, sending them to London. Any incriminating documents were now with her new solicitor, Mr William Whitby - by the way that's me, I'm the one telling this story. Her brother was at school with me. Something Samuel hated, as Henry had arranged it for services rendered by my father. Samuel thought I had risen above my station.

My father had shown me the room upon my return from America where I'd done some work for Davy Bridges, Davy had returned with me thinking he was to holiday. He hadn't liked what he'd seen. I'm now explaining this to Charlotte and to you the reader. Charlotte is recouping on her family's little island just off the estuary, about 10 miles from Mayfield her home town. We're all sitting on the dock with our feet in the water. She has many questions and we're all trying to answer them hoping she'll find some peace.

I look at her and smile and she blushes - but we can leave that story for another time.

A Physical Presence

by Zofia Ellis

This is an extract from the beginning of a debut novel in progress.

February 14th 1996

Dusk was falling as Miles Bailey turned his Land Rover Discovery into the drive of his country cottage on the edge of the village of Woodstone, a few miles from Stratford upon Avon. He hesitated before turning his engine off, listening to the last waves rolling away on *Sittin' on the Dock of the Bay*, the Otis Redding CD he had put on to clear his head on the way up from London. The cottage looked warm and welcoming. Albert had lit a fire with apple logs and left some lights on. The resulting glow poured out into the cold twilight and filled the air with sweet wood smoke.

He checked the hall table for post, found none and shook his head. Not one Valentine's card, not even from his secretary Natasha.

"Perhaps next year when I'm thirty-seven, even older," he thought, as he attempted to make himself a drink. Not the easiest of tasks. Albert, his long serving housekeeper, was incredibly faithful but very forgetful and was a little unmethodical in his storage of necessary household items which meant that Miles could never find a thing.

"I wonder where Albert's put the Jim Beam today. The kitchen perhaps?" he said out loud to himself as he opened various doors. "The broom cupboard? The fridge? The freezer? Ah, of course, here it is, in the larder behind the flour!"

Sitting in his armchair by the fire with his drink, he reached underneath the chair to retrieve his packet of Disque Bleu French cigarettes. Numerous attempts to give up smoking had forced Miles to hide the dreaded packets from himself, but he'd remembered where he had stashed these. That discovery combined with Albert's misplacing of things around the house meant that to sit comfortably with a drink and a cigarette within minutes of coming home, counted as a great success.

Relaxing in the glow of the fire, he had almost fallen asleep when his peace was interrupted by banging on the kitchen door.

"Ok, Ok, I'm coming," he muttered, opening the door to discover his bedraggled seventeen-year-old niece Nancy breathless and shaking with fright.

"What's the matter? Come in Nancy, you look dreadful." He was concerned at her appearance. Her normally pale complexion had turned chalk white. She brushed away some of her tumbling auburn hair out of her striking emerald green eyes fringed with long dark eyelashes.

"Tell me what's happened?"

"I was walking George through Woodstone Woods," she blurted.

"Well what happened? Where is he? Is he all right?"

"Yes he's in your car. You left it open again. Anyway, it started to get dark and we were still up as far as the Roman ruins, so I took a short cut through another part of the wood and I got a bit lost."

"Yes but surely George knows that spot like the back of his paw?"

"Yes I know that, but he'd gone off. I looked and looked but couldn't find him and then it got darker and then I saw her!"

"Saw whom?"

"Charlotte!" she replied. "I saw Charlotte in the woods!"

There was an almighty crash as a glass smashed onto the stone floor. Miles looked down with dismay at his empty hand to see that it was his own glass.

Miles put his trembling niece in his armchair by the fire, taking her coat off. Nancy was wearing black jeans tucked into red ankle boots and a chunky, chocolate brown sweater. He went and cleared away the broken glass and poured two more drinks.

"Here. Drink this, you'll feel better"

"Thanks. Mm it's nice," she said, still shaking. "What is it?"

"Bourbon."

He watched her sip the drink and wrapped one of his blankets around her shoulders and then downed his own glass in one swift gulp.

"Feeling better?"

"Much," she replied gratefully, brushing away some of the hair that had fallen into her eyes.

"Now," he enquired gently, "why don't you tell me what's been going on?"

"We were in the woods." She took a sip of her drink. "George had gone off chasing rabbits and I'd lost track of time."

"Mm. Daydreaming as usual I suppose."

"Well, the snowdrops were pretty and you're right, I was drifting along and I didn't notice that it was getting darker until, well until it was dark basically. I called George, but he was nowhere around and I just wasn't sure which direction the road was, or even the Hall was. I listened to see if I could hear him and then I heard some music. I knew it. I mean it sounded familiar, as if it was coming from the Hall and then I heard a woman's voice calling."

"Calling? Calling what?"

"Calling a name, *Christian* and then *Christian* again and again as if in a game of Hide and Seek. I couldn't make out where it was coming from, it was so close, and then I looked through some trees and I could see her."

"Who?"

"Like I said before, I could see Charlotte. I could see her as plain as anything."

"But you can't have done."

"I'm telling you Miles, I did, it *was* Charlotte!"

"But you'd hardly remember her," he said. "It's at least ten years since she..."

"Oh I know Miles, ten years since she vanished, went missing, disappeared without a trace, and nobody will ever tell me what happened. Well I do remember her, very clearly, if you must know and I know who I've just seen. It was her, believe me. George came running back and tripped me up and by then she'd gone."

"But how can you even remember her? You were so young."

"I was seven! Of course I can remember everything about that moment, that day, that month, that year. Everything."

"What do you remember?"

"Whitney Houston was number one in the charts for a start...*Saving All My Love for You...*"

"No, I mean yes, I think you're right, about the song. What else?"

"All sorts of things. But the funny thing is Miles, she looked exactly the same."

"Charlotte?"

"Yes."

"Describe her."

"Well she was just as slim as ever, with that lovely long baby blonde hair and a black Alice headband and she was wearing a full, black skirt with a wide belt and a black sweater with another black sweater wrapped around her shoulders."

"And you could see all of this in the dark?"

"Well sort of, but the funny thing is that was what she was wearing the last time I saw her, in fact that was just how she looked, the same clothes, the same mood.."

"Nancy? Tell me, when was the last time you saw Charlotte? Exactly?"

"Valentine's Day 1986. Ten years ago today."

"But that's on the day she disappeared."

"Yes. I remember."

"And did you see anyone else just now?"

"No. No one at all"

"Finish your drink Nancy. You'd better take me to exactly where you say you saw her."

"I did see her, honestly"

"Take your coat. I'll see you in the car. I won't be long."

Nancy did as he said, pausing briefly to bend down and pick up some stray fragments of glass that remained on the kitchen floor. She could hear Miles on the telephone.

"...You really think the siege in Sarajevo is coming to an end? I know, almost four years. Estimates at over ten thousand dead? Jesus! When do you fly? Look Christian, I understand you're leaving in a few days, but can you make it up here? Nancy tells me...Nancy? You know, my niece Nancy, is convinced that she's just seen Charlotte! When? Less than an hour ago. In the woods up by the Hall. Yes, I'm going down there with her now. Just bloody well get yourself up here as soon as you possibly can. Tonight please!"

She heard the phone go down sharply and Miles looked cross as he rushed her out of the cottage muttering, "Oh just leave that glass for Albert. Come on let's get off. Christ it's getting cold out here tonight Nancy!"

"Mm..." she agreed. "I think it might snow."

"God. That's all we need. Now where are we going, by the Hall you said?"

"Yes," she replied leaning into the back of the car

to check on George, her mother's brown and white King Charles Spaniel.

"Is he still with us?" he asked turning on the headlights and spinning the car around.

"Oh yes," she replied. "Miles, why did Charlotte go? I mean why did she just go away without telling you or anybody else?"

"I wish I knew. I really wish I knew. Straight on up here?"

"Yes."

He turned into the tiny village of Woodstone and they passed Mrs Meebie's village shop and a little farther on the left Nancy's home, The Old School House, with its white picket fence and school bell still intact and now used by her family as a very grand door bell. They approached a sharp bend out of the village and Miles hit the accelerator manoeuvring the car over the small stone bridge into the Woodstone Estate at breakneck speed.

"Christ, are you trying to kill me?" said Nancy.

"Oh be quiet and hold on tight. How much more to go?"

"Not too far. Past the gates to the Hall there's a track on the right. On the right, just here see!"

He quickly turned into the track, the moon and his headlights lighting up ranks of bare tree trunks forming the edge of Woodstone Woods.

"Look can you see, up there straight ahead, there's a bit of a clearing. Stop just there."

Miles stopped in the middle of the wood and they got out of the Discovery, letting George out at the same time and leaving the headlights shining into the trees. Nancy went on straight ahead in the direction of the beam of light from the vehicle, crunching icy twigs beneath her.

"Hang on a minute, wait for me," he called as he lost sight of her. George had begun to scamper after Nancy but had stopped to have a good sniff of the ground. Miles went up to him and bent down to give him a stroke.

"Good boy George."

George looked up at him, paused, and then loped off back towards the car.

"Oh well that's brilliant. Leave me on my own here then. Daft dog!"

He followed the ever dwindling beam of headlights until it faded out and he was faced with more trees in the moonlight. He was cold and wrapped his coat tighter across his chest. He could sense the trees in his way and gingerly held his arms ahead of him to avoid bumping into any of them. The wood was silent and he hadn't got very far when he heard a twig snap in front of him and slowly inching his way forward in the darkness, came across Nancy leaning her shoulder against a tree. She sensed him approach.

"There you are Nancy," he complained. "That George of yours is as much use as…"

She put her arm out to stop him.

"Ssh Miles. Listen!" They stood silently together for a while. George returned and muzzled up to Nancy. Miles gave him a mock sneering sideways glance. After what seemed to him to be an interminable few minutes of silence, Miles began to shuffle.

"I can't hear a bloody thing Nancy."

"No Miles, wait," she said softly. "Trust me. Just listen very carefully and keep looking straight ahead."

Through the still night air the faintest few notes of a piano began to drift towards them.

"Over there. Look," she whispered.

Among the shadows of the trees they could just about make out the slim silhouette of a young woman. As their eyes adjusted to the dim light, she became ever clearer. Long blonde hair, just as Nancy had described, she was nonchalantly looping her arm around a tree and then swinging around looping her arm around another and then pausing, called gently, "Christian," and then again, "Christian."

"Charlotte!" shouted Miles as he ran towards her.

The moon slipped back behind a shelf of clouds and the gentlest fall of huge snowflakes began to float down from the sky. Nancy couldn't see either of them and the wood was silent again. Standing still and her face bathed by snowflakes, she stroked George.

"Come on George, we may as well go back to the car, we'll freeze out here."

By the time they reached the car, the snow had already settled on the bonnet. She watched the snowflakes slowly sink past through the headlights of the car, wondering why it was that falling snow somehow made the quietest of nights seem even quieter. After a while she saw the dark shape of Miles coming back through the trees. He ran his fingers through his damp hair.

"Come on Nance, let's go." He paused and said in

a quiet, sad voice, "I lost her."

They got back in the car and Nancy could see that his face looked worn and drawn.

"Right." He started the car and turned out of the clearing and out of the wood.

"Where are we going?" she asked, brushing snowflakes off her sleeves.

"Up here I think, I need a drink," he replied turning the car into the drive of Woodstone Hall Hotel.

"I haven't been her for ages."

"No, me neither. Not since the new owners took over."

The snow had fallen quite deeply now and they made virgin tracks in the drive edged by rhododendrons turning whiter by the second. Miles glided the car around a bend, and Woodstone Hall appeared grandly floodlit through the thickening snowflakes over the lake before them. They drove over the stone balustrade bridge at the edge of the lake and approached the Hall, passing a smaller solitary building in darkness on their left, the Chapel.

"Oh wow, don't those rooms upstairs look gorgeous!" said Nancy.

As it was still early in the evening, the curtains of the bedrooms had yet to be drawn and they opulently draped the sides of each window revealing the tops of romantic four poster beds.

"We'll take George with us, he'll freeze in here," said Miles as he parked the car.

They walked through the falling snow and he opened the heavy wooden doors.

The sheer scale of the recent restoration of the Hotel overwhelmed Miles and stunned his senses. From the heavily scented china bowls of pot-pourri, to the warmth from the logs crackling away in the huge hall fireplace. Perfect paintings hung in perfectly appointed places. Glossy magazines surrounded large pots of white orchids on antique circular tables and the light from expensive table lamps shone on the polished stone floor. He smiled wistfully remembering what it had been like before.

"I remember a room full of vinyl covered club chairs, books and…well not much else really. Christian used to bring us all here for afternoon tea every now and again, and we would be incredibly rude to the staff. Talking of which, I'll go and find someone and organise a drink and then I want a word with you…"

"Oh dear." She concentrated on the magazines on the table.

Nancy stared at the ice cubes in her glass of cider, with George asleep at her feet, in the room Miles had mentioned. It was now comfortably filled with real leather chairs and expansive wall to wall bookcases.

"Tell me, just when exactly was the last time you saw Charlotte?"

"Apart from just now?"

"Apart from just now." He lit a cigarette.

"I remember it so clearly. It was as if… as if it was just now really. In fact that was exactly the way she looked, the same clothes, the same mood."

"What do you mean?"

"She was so happy, so very, very happy."

"Where were you?"

"In Woodstone. I'd just come out of Mrs Meebie's shop with some sweets for me and the *Sporting Life* for Albert."

"That man and his bloody horses!"

"I know. Anyway, she stopped in that lovely car of hers."

"The primrose E Type?"

"Yes. She had the hood down, it was so cold that day too. She asked me how I was, she was always so nice to me."

"What did she talk about?"

"Well, we were leaving to go skiing that night. Don't you remember Mum and Dad were taking me to Kitzbuhel?"

"Of course, that's right, you were all away in Austria that year. Are you certain, about the day?"

"Yes. That's why she was there. I mean that's what she was so happy about. She told me she'd received a Valentine's card that morning arranging a…how did she put it? Oh, a *romantic tryst* up at the Hall, I mean here."

"Who from, or rather with whom?"

"I don't know. I didn't ask her and she didn't say who."

"Are you sure about that? You don't know who she was meeting?"

"Only that it was a man. Of course I'm sure. What do you sometimes call my memory – *Total Recall*, like the film?"

"Yes, yes I know, it's always been remarkable, I keep telling you." He smiled. "Carry on. What *did* she say?"

"Oh, let me think." She screwed up her face. "Well she pinched one of my chocolates and lent me one of the cassette tapes from her car."

"Oh God her awful taste in music, don't remind me." Miles laughed.

"It was not! I liked it. It was funny about the cassette though."

"Why?"

"Well the cover was Go West – I loved them. Remember their song then?" She started to quietly sing:

> *"Don't look down girl*
> *You know you're holding aces*
> *Don't look down girl*
> *Don't give the game away..."*
> *"No."*

"Oh Miles, you're such a bore!" She put her arms behind her head and pressed her lips together as she collected her thoughts. "That's about it really. Oh and she picked out a tip for Albert out of the paper. We giggled about the names. Which one was it? Mm, Rebellion I think? Oh no it wasn't that one, she finally decided on the one called Wide Boy. She told me to tell Albert to put a packet on Wide Boy and it came in as well. Twenty to one. Albert came round to the house and told me later with some toffees for me."

"Makes a change for Albert to actually win a bet," he muttered. "Anything else?"

"No I don't think so, she picked out the tips really quickly. I think she was more interested in the next day's racing really."

"She was going racing the next day? Where? Did she say? Can you remember anything else about that?

"No I'm not sure," she paused. But when I got home, I was really miffed because the tape in the box wasn't Go West after all, which was really odd because she said it had been a special present and that she'd been listening to it a real lot."

"What was it then?"

"Level 42. It was quite good. I've still got it at home somewhere."

"Level who?"

"I give up!" She pressed her knuckles into her chin and raised her eyes to the ceiling, bemused by Miles' lack of knowledge of even ten-year-old music.

"Who did you tell this to Nancy?"

"Nobody."

"For God's sake, why not?"

"Well we were away and anyway she made me promise not to tell anybody I'd seen her or that she was going to meet someone. She said goodbye and sped off in her car up the lane to the Hall."

"You're sure she didn't even hint at who she was meeting?"

"Yes. Quite sure. Honestly Miles that's all I can remember. Besides, you knew her far better than I did. Don't you have any idea who it could have been? Could it have been Christian she was meeting?"

"Christian?" he asked, surprised. "He was in America at the time doing a follow up story on the Challenger Shuttle disaster. Are you sure you saw her?"

"Yes I am!"

"But what the hell is she doing in Woodstone Woods now?"

Miles was confused by the events of the evening so far. Suddenly seeing Charlotte before his very eyes like that, only for her to disappear into the night, and Nancy's talk of the meeting in the village all those years ago. But something else was eating at him even more. He felt sick to the stomach as he recalled the words that Nancy had used to describe Charlotte: *In fact that was just the way she looked, the same clothes, the same mood.*

Meeting Up

by Keith Myers

I am taking the bus with my pass,
on the Coastliner I travel to Malton and Scarborough mass
as we travel, admire the views,
I get chatting to an attractive lady with nice shoes
as we chat we love the scenery and nice weather
we exchange names, hers is Heather.
The time seems to fly,
and we exchange phone numbers to keep in touch.

Arriving in Scarborough, we go for a walk & chat away as such,
admiring the sea, sand & boats.
There is quite a few people about and no coats.
After lockdown, it is nice to see people having fun
what next ice cream and some nice sun.
Taking it all in we sit on the seafront
watching the boats and a punt,
then off we go chatting away like old friends do,
we take a break and dash to the loo.

On our way back we look around the shops.
We head for the bus and say the day has been tops.
On the way back, Heather, and I say lets keep in touch,
we agree it would mean so much.
Since we have been back we have met and Heather

looks so nice.
It could be a short romance,
but engagement has every chance.
Marriage next, what else can there be
let's hope for the best and see
There is now time to get everything ready for the big day.
Dreams can come true you just don't know what to say
This was a meeting made to happen for us,
Let's see where it goes, from that meeting on the bus.

Church of the Green Cross

by Michael Fairclough

I'm a petty criminal and thinking about it, that's how all this started. Waiting outside a school one day on my moped, looking for a target. She was a mum pushing a pram with her child she had just picked up from school.

"Perfect." I revved my moped and set off down the grass verge at the side of the road. Getting close, I reached out for the child's bag of sweets that his mum had presumably bought to pacify them on the way home. Then I dropped onto the road and up to the zebra crossing. Unfortunately, I was not paying attention and, no, there were no children on the crossing. But there was a lollipop man stopping traffic for a hedgehog. Which regrettably halted my escape as I skidded off the spikey rat and was launched over my handles.

Out of hospital I found myself with a suspended sentence, ordered to do unpaid work as a dinner lady. (Dinner man? Dinner Lord or maybe Dinner Baron - then again the Lord of Dinner isn't too bad either.) Reluctantly I complied, figuring if I made a fuss the judge may make me do something even more tedious and deafening than serve children their lunch. (Seriously, I forgot how loud them lunch halls could get!) So I showed up everyday and helped cook and feed the kids. Of course I did find a way to make it fun eventually, as I began to steal as much as I could from the kitchen. Plastic lunch trays up my shirt, knives, forks and spoons in my pockets or the odd rolling pin shoved down the front of my boxers.

Anyhow, that's not what this is about. As all my time at the school got me thinking. It's weird how you can grow out of things not by choice but by simply not needing them anymore, like newspapers and television were always around in my childhood but now? My dad still has a television, but that's in part ignorance to the benefits of a good computer. The amount of time he spends flicking trying to find something to watch that is not just finishing and that's interesting, he could be downloading or streaming a new film or commencing a box set. As for newspapers: again, he still reads them and is presented with the same problem, just in a different context. Then again, newspaper websites are horrible places full of adverts, opinion pieces, celeb gossip, fluff and the sport section, which I just don't see as pertinent information, next to the funerals and that one reporters obsession with local dogging sites. (Sorry, bit of a rant there.) So it was with this line of thinking, and me being back in a school. I noticed all the things I no longer use. Completely unremarkable things for an adult to no longer think about. Like the tiny urinals they install so the boys can reach, or the lollipop people. (Which is weird as they are pretty hard to miss.) Only at their station when school opens and lets out. So where do they go? This in mind, one lunchtime I decided, screw it, I would follow one. Allowing the rest of my shift to fly by, I daydreamed about how the lollipop person probably just feeds ducks or has a mild gambling habit. Either way, I thought to myself, if it turned out to be a boring confrontation, I still had my cutlery theft to fall back on for thrills. I slid two clean forks into my back pockets and rammed a beige tray up under my t-shirt, before tucking the shirt in and replacing my school-provided apron over the top.

Done for the day, I made my way out of the school and headed to the staff car park. At my moped, I put as much of my treasure in my top box over the back wheel as I could. I was going to have to empty it soon though, as not everything would fit in. I'd already stolen all the ladles and spatulas that morning then used a smoke break as cover to ditch them. That done, I headed around to the school gates to find my target. Stood in a tired posture, the man held his lollipop with both hands around the shaft. Not on duty yet. You could tell he hated the children or was at least fed up with them as he dawdled in place waiting for the bell to signify the end of school. Speak of the devil.

"Rinnnnnnnng." The man tensed, stood straight, slapped himself then painted on a grin. It's always the same: the quiet before the storm, then gradually the building talks in unintelligible gossip and taunting, as the children make their way out of their last classes for the day. Some getting school buses, others crossing the road to get the service bus, and the more local children walking home with a friend. The man went about his business, all the while that forced smile drooping lower and lower and dipping into the red at one point when a boy on a bike rammed his shin before cycling off with his waiting cronies. He was the last though, it seemed, so the man dropped the act and threw up a finger to the now distant cyclists, before stretching and wondering off in the other direction.

"Finally." I gasped as I copied him and stretched, having been squatting behind a black council bin at the bus stop for long enough to get pins and needles when I stood up. Having failed to shake it off though, I found myself having to follow him with my leg still slightly numb, giving me a odd limp, but I refused to lose track. A short walk later and the man had stopped at a different bus stop. Annoyed, I tried to ignore the pointlessness, since he could have caught the same bus up at the school. Realizing he would have probably found me behind the bin though, I brushed off my grievance and approached. Slowly getting closer with each step so as not to startle the wizened man, until I got close enough it was apparent I was getting the bus. Both faced forward, lingering like someone waiting for the toilet, except in this case it was a bus.

Around fifteen minutes later, a double decker pulled up. I let him go first; he paid in coins and placed his lollipop on the baggage rack before going upstairs. It didn't matter though: as long as I was downstairs there was only one way off. (Well, unless he had one of them tiny red emergency hammers.) Things soon took a turn however - literally and physically - as we took a sharp corner and stopped to pick up two more lollipop people. One was a small man carrying a caged animal, the other a hard-faced elderly woman. (Which is saying something, as they all seem quite old.) She paid for herself and her colleague, before leaving him downstairs with the lollipops.. and his pet? A few stops later the bus was getting to be standing room only, partly due to several more commuters getting on and partly due to three more lollipop people. Another pair and then a single just before town. Nodding at one another, they then stood in silence until the bus passed the hospital where they turned in unison on the chime of the buses bell. Stopping, they disembarked and I watched as legs appeared on the stairs of the lollipop woman followed by my original lollipop man. The group now all off, I ditched my copy of the metro I had cut eyeholes into with my keys on the seat next to me. Then tried my best to act casual as I briskly walked to the doors.

The lollipop people were organised as they made their way to the nearest crossing before I even stepped off the bus, and just like parting the red sea the cars stopped flowing on their command and then resumed behind the last, leaving me stranded on the wrong side of the road. This was a problem, as when I got there the button for the lights was out of order. Watching them from across the road I tried my best to see what door they went into, but it being a side street the numbers where obscured from me and, on the man finally turning green of its own accord, I was worried it was too late. Once at the other side, I jogged to the street the lollipop people went down, but they were nowhere to be seen. A different one was, though, and made his presence known to me with a smoker's cough. Sat on a wall in an alcove of sorts partitioning the doors from a bike and lollipop rack, the lollipop man looked at me.

"New blood, green blood or red blood?" he questioned.

"Red blood?" I replied not sure if a quiz or some sort of test.

"Oh fantastic, don't see it often here but I'm glad some people know what to do. Go on in, through door, down the stairs then it's the door on the left. Then again there is only one door. Oh well I'm sure you will figure it out. In fact, I will be with you in a second, just got to finish this." He gestured to an exterior door with his cigarette then at his cigarette with his other hand. Puzzled at his question and my answer, I went along with his instructions and opened the door to the stairs. That's when I noticed the noise emanating from the building, partially drowned out by the traffic outside but getting louder at every step. Familiar rumbling and clattering, yet I could not place it. Hesitant, I stood halfway down the stairs when darkness covered me. Turning around the lollipop man was behind me his lollipop blocking out the afternoon sun.

"Were you waiting for me? How sweet, go on, I'm with you now - just like crossing the road." I continued down the stairs. No way out, I got to the bottom and opened the door slowly, hoping it would not groan. The door not creaking, I was relived until on the other side, as the internal noise gradually stopped. Now, let me tell you, there is nothing quite like the feeling of being out of place, the odd one out, and this was very much a case of it. The room was full of lollipop men and women playing snooker. Was this some sort of club or gathering? I could not tell you, but the way they looked at me while brandishing their lollipops sent chills down my spine. I was not welcome, that was clear, and I raised my hand, about to tell them I would go, I think I have the wrong place - when a lone rumble began. Turning to the sound, I found it had stopped and a ball was on its way to my face at great speed.

"Shi--"

I was pulled up straight and supported either side by hands grasping my arms. Thankfully I was not tied or cuffed. A small win, but I was blind folded. That could be temporary though, as a precaution so I could not see where we were heading. My only clue was that we were going deeper. My body recognized the sensation of walking down an incline and the coldness of a cellar or underground station. On arriving, my vision was restored and a bag tossed to the floor in front of me before I was forced to kneel, which allowed me to take in the lollipop people's lair in awe. Fashioned from an old sewer, the roof was curved in old brick and clad in pipes and tubes along its length before separating into nooks, crannies and an endless unlit tunnel. Speechless, I stared around. I had plenty of time to, as I was seemingly not a priority. A congregation engaged in a line dance and chanting on a zebra crossing that acted as a central isle between pavements either side and gutters stained a rusty brown leading to a dais, but more so pedestrian.

That's when the lighting of the church directly above caught my eye. A chandelier with an intricate zebra framing leading out to small belisha beacons causing the church to be draped in a sickly orange glow. Well except for one thing I almost completely passed over: inset in the back wall behind the altar was a small green 'x' that glowed faintly. Almost as if it was the most unremarkable thing there. I could tell it was important, however, as two lollipop people guarded it at either side, their high visibility jackets being the thing that drew me to them – well, that and them being adorned with zebra skins, covering their heads and their lollipops held ready to swat anyone who got too close. Taking in the room further only cemented my opinion as I found the symbol depicted everywhere as a decorative touch. Almost as if an icon, it was engraved as a centrepiece in all its locations, drawing your focus, and in one such case it was held aloft by two little men, one red and one green.

While I'd been distracted, the dance had ended, quiet filling the space the way as only it can.

"Blood of the zebra!" a female voice shouted. Snapping my head around I found the source. A lollipop lady had taken to the dais. A thin woman, whose high visibility jacket gave the appearance of bulk. The illusion was broke though due to her choice of head garment. As like the others she had a pelt draped over her. A dead squirrel.

"Blood of the zebra!" the room responded with even my guards impassioned at the chant.

"Blood of the squirrel!"

"Blood of the squirrel!"

"Blood for the Emerald Man who sleeps eternal!"

"Blood for the Emerald Man who sleeps eternal!"

At that they erupted in a vague shout, stamping and banging their lollipops on the ground. Probably my best chance, so I took it and reached into my pockets. My fingers were just long enough to wiggle the forks up and grasp them. Primed in my hand, I then stretched enough to un-tuck my shirt, releasing the dinner tray I had stuffed up there earlier. It fell faster than expected; however, it forced me to make my move sooner rather than later. So as my guards attention turned on me I jerked free of their elderly and frankly quite weak grasps before stabbing them in the legs with the forks. One went deep and took its target down with ease; the other not as effective, turning out to be a spoon I pocketed by mistake. Improvising, I lunged away to buy time. His grip was practically non-existent now. His speed, however, was deadly as an inch to the left my head would have rolled, cut off by the razor edge of his lollipop. My turn: I pounced forward, closing the distance in seconds before grabbing the back of his head to steady him, then scooping out his eye with my stolen spoon.

"Argh!" The man cried out, alerting the flock to my attack and causing their convergence on me. Picking up one of the lollipops and the tray I stole, I fled and headed back the way I'd been led, which was pretty much a straight path back up the underground hill. A short run later I seemed to arrive back at the snooker hall as the sound of balls clattered around behind a closed door. My pursuers at my back however, I found myself trapped. My only options both involved confrontation.

"Sod it." I barged through the door. Taking notice at my brashness, some occupants immediately made for me. The maze-like layout of the tables only served to slow them down though, as the entrance was width-ways for me rather than lengthwise. It left only a handful of them to deal with, brandishing their lollipops with intent to do harm. Taking to the tables I figured the high ground would be an advantage as I leaped ever closer to the ones at the last table. Landing, they swung at me, one overhead and one from either side at my chest and feet. Thinking fast, I jumped back and down off the table, causing all to miss me – but not to miss my attackers, as the two swipes took each other out at least temporarily. This left only one, which hit the table due to my absence and began to shake, as the shockwave ran up his lollipop and back into his body. His violence paused, I swung my lollipop at him, flat side hitting him like a giant slap, causing his high visibility hat to fly off and land on a coat hook. Him out of the way, I was back on the table and off the other side then out the door that my curiosities had led me astray through.

Running up the stairs I saw daylight - well, the scraps of it, evening having set in while I was underground - but that was not all to see, as the lollipop man who was smoking before greeted me, balanced on the same wall. He was a guard, I thought, his position clicking into place. We eyed each other before he threw his cigarette to the ground and went for his lollipop. I was already in a one-armed swing with my plastic lunch tray and hit his face before he could even grasp his shaft, his head moving faster than his hand as it cracked against the brick wall next to the door, before the man fell backwards unconscious over his perch. My tray now cracked, I ditched it, chucking it on the lifeless lollipop man before remembering my pursuers. I barred the door with my stolen lollipop. Eager now to get away and slightly annoyed I did not shout dinner time when I wacked the man, I took off with a sprint back to the bus stop.

Luck not on my side I could see the bus, but it was stuck in roadwork.

Arriving back at the school it had gotten dark. I pressed the bell and walked to the doors as the bus slowed down for the stop. Getting off I thanked the driver and walked over to the now unmanned zebra crossing. Letting the bus pass, I discovered a queue had formed behind it. So waiting for the traffic to thin, my eyes wandered, landing on the crossing. Hit suddenly with a sick feeling, my stomach dropped at what I had witnessed and what was still smeared across one of the zebra's white stripes. Gagging I looked back to see only one visible car.

"After this." I said, getting ready as the cars headlights lit up the darkness on either side of the road, and a figure in yellow waiting opposite me that I had not noticed until then. Panicked, I ran across the road in a direct line to where I had parked - only to discover what it's like to be a hedgehog.

Back in hospital I was somewhat relieved, thinking that my escapade had been nothing but a guilt-ridden dream for killing that darned spikey rat after I robbed that kid. On glancing to the door I found a policeman guarding my room. Curious of the time, I scanned the area for a clock and found one next to me on a bedside table.

"Half twelve, I could eat." Fortunately it would seem the nurses agreed, as on making the remark a man came in with a trolley of food. Smiling at me the man loaded a cracked beige tray with the usual hospital atrocities, then handed it to me and left without uttering a word. Opting to eat the sandwich first, I picked up the limp triangle and brought it to my mouth for a bite. But once through the bread, my teeth were greeted with an odd texture, which on escaping from the sandwich stabbed at my mouth's soft interior. Spitting out the food onto the tray I examined the inside of the sandwich. But there was no identifiable fillings or spreads, just what appeared to be the spikes of a hedgehog. Disgusted I flung the remainder of the sandwich across the room, hitting the back of the policeman's head.

"Ouch!"

Then I reached for the glass of orange that accompanied my inedible assailant. Swigging half the glass I tried not to retch at what I had just had in my mouth, only for the tray to demand my attention again. Since what I had spat up was not alone.

In between the chewed up quills and bread was what appeared to be a human eye looking back at me.

Instructions on Making Quilts...the English Method

by Stuart Hillard

"The origins of the patchwork quilt are murky but even those with the slightest interest should be able to make the distinction between the American and the English methods of construction. English Patchwork Quilts are most distinct from their American cousins, being made from small pieces of many assorted fabrics which have first been folded over and tacked to very accurately cut heavy paper shapes, often hexagons or some other geometric shape. Quilts contain the scraps and rags and childhood clothes, the hopes and aspirations of the maker. Her secrets and the stories are stitched into every seam."

One

Gather your materials

You will need thick paper for templates, old envelopes work well. The best kind come from a bundle of old letters found on the day of your mother's funeral, tied with ribbon, yellowed with age and frayed at the ends but holding their secrets tight. Choose fabrics in a variety of cheerful prints to make your patchwork sing. Cherished clothes, (often children's) can be used. If you can, find a lace edged handkerchief to add in, embroidered with a bunch of cornflowers and stained with tears. If you come across a butter yellow pinafore dress you don't remember wearing, lovingly wrapped in tissue and tucked in a faded box, so much the better. Cotton fabrics work best, but consider adding plain white or cream calico to give the pretty scraps space to breathe. Finally, pins, needle and thread. Use pins and needles that are sharpened from years of use, pins that were held in a mothers mouth as she hissed at you to "stand still", needles drawn through fabric at the fireside and parked in a skirt when the kettle boiled, thread that is strong. Strong enough to hold the fragments together, thread that will not break, even when you tug it in anger or pain.

My mother's stroke had been catastrophic, destroying her brain like a carelessly dropped match ripping through a barn full of barley straw. There had been no smoulder, there had been no smoke.

I had been staying with her on the old family farm for almost a week, a brief respite from my city life and a chance to clear my head after weeks of stress and problems at work. Mother had not made a fuss when I arrived, neither surprised by my unexpected arrival nor disappointed or perturbed. She had merely tipped her chin in my direction and raised her eyebrows. Then she did what she always did in uncomfortable situations, she put the kettle on for tea. Within the hour she had me in boots a size too small, weeding an onion patch with her in silence which might have been mistaken for companionable had it not been for our history. It was Wednesday and we had fed the chickens that morning as we had on the other five preceding days, 6am, just as the sun rose. I had crawled out of bed, the city girl in me needing a cigarette and a Berocca chaser but the country girl in me knowing neither was an option. Instead I pulled the faded nine-patch quilt off my bed and wrapped myself in it, taking me to the barn. There was a battered tin bucket on my mother's strong and weathered forearm filled with chicken feed but she kept a handful of corn in her right pocket as a treat for her special girls. I leaned against the peeling doorframe of the chicken barn and watched as she dipped her free hand into the pail and cast handfuls onto the floor. It was a strangely nurturing act to see my mother perform and it confused me and made me smile in equal measure. I laughed at the chickens' merry dance as they picked every one of the pellets up as fast as they fell like dun coloured rain but she never cracked her face, it was always set like stone. I collected eggs into the soft folds of my gathered apron, the smooth tan shells heavy against my bare legs and glanced across at her. Mothers head bobbed forward and back as she walked, her elbows stuck out like wings and her skinny tanned legs were shoved into heavy boots which scratched and scoured their way through the straw that carpeted the chicken house. I let out a loud cluck and laughed, her gaze flew at me, beady and sharp. "Why are you wearing my quilt like a coat?" she yelled. "You have any idea how long they take me to make?" I shook my head, mollified like a child. "Of course you don't...you're never here! And who are you sniggering at, hmm? "she said, her voice cracking like a whip, "something funny?" I smiled at her despite her harsh tone...she often sounded so abrasive when she spoke to me but I always tried to soften her edges. "I just...well I thought... you look just like one of the chickens scratching your way through the straw...going to lay me an egg?" I said trying to make her laugh. Her face didn't change, her mouth remained a thin pale line. "No Susan, I am not...go into the house and get me some gloves will you, I need to pull this ivy down, it's growing into the henhouse and it'll end up causing a leak. I know you think farm work is all a big joke but it isn't, there's nothing funny here." I shrugged and took the last egg from its cosy bed of straw and tucked it into my apron with the others. I pushed the door of the chicken barn open and walked out into the early morning sunshine and across to the house. I'd only been gone for a couple of minutes but when I returned my Mother was sprawled on the ground like a dropped doll, her eyes almost closed and her mouth, always such a straight line was dropped to one side and dribbling. The chickens were pecking at the pocket she kept the corn in and for a second I caught myself laughing and then stopped. There was nothing funny here.

I'd left her bedroom till last. I had spent most of the remainder of my planned fortnight sorting, tearlessly, through the house, organising her funeral and feeding animals but something stopped me going into her bedroom, old habits die hard I suppose. It hadn't always been her room or even her farm. As a small child it had been my grandmothers and we had spent the Summers here, Mother and I until one day we had suddenly stopped. I didn't recall why and I had certainly never dared to ask. My grandmother had died when I was eight, we hadn't gone to the funeral. I had been sent to my room for most of the day, the constant rain the only sound to drown out my parents shouting at each other. A month after her death I had at last returned to the farm with my mother and father and they had never left again. It was now the day of my mother's funeral and I had needed something to occupy me until the car came to take us both to the parish church for her burial. I had been awake since four, laying motionless in my childhood bed. I'd spent the best part of an hour staring at the ceiling and the constellations of faintly glowing plastic stars my father had placed there for me. After he'd died my primary school teacher had told me that he was one of the stars now and I'd tried so hard to imagine which one he would be. I'd settled on the Great Bear which although I knew was a group of stars and Miss Cross had told me Father was only one, I couldn't help but think of his strong and fuzzy arms gripping me tightly and I just knew that he was all of them. Mother's bedroom had always been out of bounds after that, a sanctuary away from me she had called it, a place for her to be alone with her thoughts. I had sometimes heard her crying and wondered if it was for herself, or my father, lost in a farming accident two years after our arrival or a life she might have preferred perhaps? I didn't know, I hadn't asked. There had been moments when I had wanted to burst through her stony defences and comfort her, but the moat around my mother was dug deep, the drawbridge raised, the locks firmly bolted.

The box took me by surprise. I had found it in my mother's room, tucked beneath her old oak sleigh bed, almost completely hidden by the large turkey red and white appliqué quilt which hung down to the floor. The quilt was one of my mother's; sewing quilts was, in her words, her only folly but her work was flawless. Huge spiky "princess" feathers were picked out in plain red fabric the colour of rubies and spun out from the centre of the quilt creating a huge whirling centrepiece. Around this medallion were more appliquéd feathers which created a circular frame. The crisp contrast of plain red on a white background was timeless and striking and I suddenly realised that I had never seen it actually finished and on the bed. I was almost lost in admiration for my mothers work when I spotted a box, the size of a child's suitcase, tucked beneath the bed. The box was the kind you might buy for keepsakes, it was covered in faded floral paper, pink roses and sprigs of forget-me-knots with little fancy brass corners and a matching handle. The lid lifted up with a sigh. In the box was a tiny sundress the colour of freshly churned butter, hand sewn with tiny pearl buttons down the centre. It was wrapped in fragile tissue paper, yellowed like an old map. My mother had made me a blue dress just like this but I didn't remember this yellow version. It must have been one I wore as a baby. There was a handkerchief, still crisply white and folded into a triangle, edged with lace and embroidered with tiny blue flowers. Beneath these things was a fragment of handsewn patchwork, tiny hexagons in a myriad of colourful floral scraps, still basted to their paper core, awaiting my mother's skilful hand. It was like my own quilt but this was half made. It was so unlike her not to finish something.

And then I found a bundle of letters.

They were tied with ribbon, once a bright and glossy white now aged the colour of ripening corn, the ends, once scythed at neat angles had started to unravel. There were six letters in the sheaf, all housed in identical white envelopes and the top one bore my mother's name, Dorothy Brownlow and the address was the one we had lived in before my grandmother's death, before we had moved to the farm. The ribbon was tied neatly into a bow and although it had clearly not been untied for many years it yielded at my encouraging touch and the sheaf of letters slid apart. Each one was identical but written exactly a week apart...six letters, six weeks and the most striking thing about them was that they were all unopened. I turned the earliest one over and ran the tip of my finger along the edge when I heard a gentle cough at the door and then a tap, "Miss Brownlow, it's Derek Rowbotham, the funeral director... are you ready? I knocked the door but there was no answer... I hope you don't mind." His voice was soft, almost feminine, practised in the art of comforting people gripped by sadness and loss. I swallowed hard and returned the envelope to its hiding place; its contents would have to wait until later. "Yes Mr Rowbotham, I'm ready."

Two

Prepare your patches

Cut out hexagons from your thick paper... cut as many patches as you require at the start. Each patch in your quilt will need its own paper template so make tea or pour wine, this will take a while. As you make the templates don't forget to read the letters and to piece together the fragments of your history but be prepared for the truths you've lived by to be cut to size and the memories you hold so dear to be reformed into a new design. It's usually best to launder the fabrics before you cut them but this means letting go of the fragrance of lavender mixed with sweat and your grandmother's house and summer holidays... and rain.

Cut the fabric patches a little bigger than your paper templates, a ¼ inch is perfect. Thread a needle with 18" of sewing cotton, any colour will do bar red, which can run like a river of blood so choose it at your peril. Pin the paper template to the back of the fabric patch and carefully fold the extra fabric over the edge then use the needle and thread to baste or tack the fabric to the paper. Keep the corners neat and use big running stitches to hold the edges down. Prepare all your patches in this way. You will probably need a cosy fire and music that reminds you of the past and perhaps even a friend to help you...with the stitching and trying to piece the memories together as they come tumbling out and to make sense of it all.

I had meant to read the letters that very same night but I had not returned from the funeral alone. My cousin Rita had sat with me in the tiny parish church throughout the service holding my hand at moments she thought appropriate and squeezing them firmly when she thought I needed extra comfort. She was only a couple of years older than me, but she looked middle aged, careworn but homely. The sort of person who would make you tea and tell you that things would get better. She had smiled at me and whispered that I looked distant. "Thinking about Mum, are you?" she'd asked and nodded kindly. She was a nurse on an Alzheimer's ward and was good at this sort of thing, comforting the dying and the bereaved. The truth was I had spent the whole time wondering who the trio of women sitting on the opposite side of the aisle were. They were dressed in bright colours and resembled a flock of exotic birds, all feathers and watchful eyes and chatter. The taller and more striking of the trio had been the only person to perform a eulogy, and had talked about my mother so lovingly and warmly that for a moment I questioned if I had got my timings wrong and this was someone else's funeral. I didn't have to wonder who they were for too long: as soon as I stepped out in the bright August sunshine they had swooped. The tall one introduced them all - Sarah, Gwen and Lucy - and explained that they were the three remaining members of my mother's Friday night quilting group. She explained that they'd been meeting at the farm for almost twenty years.

"Your mother was like a sister to us, wasn't she girls?" Sarah had said to the other two. Sarah seemed to be the ringleader of the group, she was perhaps eighty and unusually tall and slender with wild silver hair swept up onto the top of her head, with what remained of her original copper tones spun through it like threads of gold. She wore a vivid chartreuse green velvet jacket which was tailored to her elegant shoulders, and beneath it she wore a flaming copper silk dress and a necklace of huge and highly polished amber beads. "Your mother formed our little quilting group just after you left University and moved to London. We met every week without fail until a fortnight ago. We talked more than we quilted of course..." Her voice trailed off as she looked me up and down. "She was so very proud of you, Susan." Sarah's words stung me like the flick of a riding crop. I felt my eyes smart and shook my head, "That doesn't sound like my mother at all Miss..."

"You can call me Sarah, my dear," the woman said. "We really should get together while you're still at the house, shouldn't we girls?" She looked at her two companions, Gwen and Lucy, who I had only just realised were identical twins. They had taken such lengths to disguise the fact that I hadn't realised it at first. The women both nodded in unison.

"We really--" started Gwen,

"—should," finished Lucy.

"We really should," they both said together and smiled at me with beaming, innocent and almost childish faces. I smiled and shook my head.

"I don't know, ladies, I'm leaving at the end of the week, I have to get back to London for work." Sarah rested an amber ringed hand on my forearm and fixed me with eyes the colour of opals.

"Nonsense," she said, "we will make time. Tomorrow at 4. The girls will bake." She nodded at the twin sisters who smiled even more broadly. I walked back to the farm with Rita, my head a swirl of amber beads and green velvet, patchwork quilts and a cherished yellow dress I was sure wasn't mine but most of all a bundle of letters I couldn't wait to open and read.

Blind Bride

by Mary C Palmer

Everything was whizzing around in my head; my sister was upsetting the other bridesmaid, I couldn't find all of the page boys' outfits, my mother was snapping at me about how I should not wear my makeup; no one was happy at all.

I was trying to fix everything, and this just distracted me from thinking about myself and the things I wanted and didn't want. I was just trying to keep all the plates spinning in the air, petrified that one might fall and smash to the ground; smashing the whole lot with it and creating a disaster. Relatives were arriving and at that moment I was full of surprise and smiles and welcoming them.

Then the house began to quietly settle til there was suddenly no more noise. They had all gone to the church and I realised I hadn't brushed my teeth! So, there I am, in my wedding dress, brushing my teeth and being so afraid of getting any on my dress or ruining my makeup.

So, all is done and I'm rushing down the stairs because the car to take me and my dad to the church has arrived.

I stepped into the living room thinking the view of his beautiful daughter in her wedding dress would take his breath away - but no, not even a smile.

He just said, "You don't have to go through with this, you know, if you don't want to."

And why didn't I say, 'No Dad, I don't want to'?

But I immediately thought of all the people sitting in the church waiting for me to arrive …. All the food prepared, all the money spent and the overwhelming feeling that this was the part I played in all of this. I was petrified.

I said, "No Dad, it's all right." Not knowing what else to do, I just followed my dad and we got in the car.

We got to the church, my arm in Dad's arm and as the music started we began to walk down the aisle just as the tears began to run down my face.

Dad said, "Why are you crying?"

I said the first thing I could think of to make another plate spin in the air not wanting it to smash and break into a million pieces-

I said, "Oh it's because I'm happy."

I wasn't thinking about me at all, about my future and what I was letting myself in for, at the tender young age of 18. Whenever anyone put him down, saying how thin he was, it made me defend and protect him all the more. That's my nature anyway, I would naturally defend anyone, be it a person or a wounded animal.

He moaned about and criticised my mum and dad, saying he was going to give me a far better life and how much happier I was going to be, and this was just another plate spinning around inside my head.

Then we got to the altar and there he was, wearing a purple shirt with white stitching around the edges and I thought OMG what are you wearing, this is supposed to be your wedding day, not a frigging disco!

So the priest says, "Who gives this woman...?"

My dad says, "I do."

I turned to give my wedding bouquet to the chief bridesmaid, who was my best friend, Joyce. My sister was the other bridesmaid. She was very angry and resented me for giving the grand title of Chief Bridesmaid to Joyce rather than bestowing her with the title; she so resented Joyce for taking the position that she felt was hers.

The tension between them could have been cut with a knife.

It just added to all the mixed up, unhappy feelings I was feeling anyway.

Like it was all my fault. As if I had failed in some way, failed to spin this plate and keep it in the air. More importantly, it was another distraction from me thinking about myself and the reality of what I was entering into.

So, turning back to the priest with all this spinning around in my mind, I tried to remember to repeat the vows after the priest.

I heard, "I now pronounce you man and wife."

Where was the excitement in that moment?

I felt so bewildered; I was just following through with the role that had been set before me and was expected of me by the families and the congregation.

We were shuffled along to a little room to sign the register and I'm still not feeling it. I hoped, things would liven up at the reception when the music started and everyone is dancing and so, off down the aisle we go.

The black and white photographs ae shot in the school playground with neighbours' back gardens the background to my wedding photos

The wind is blowing a gale and my veil covers my face, feeling like it's going to leave and take off any minute. My wedding bouquet in one hand, trying to move the veil away from my face with the other, I look at my family. None of them seem to be enjoying this supposedly happy occasion that I'm playing the main role in, and it was all for them.

I just don't get it.

The photographer has done his job, and I'm walking across the school playground and into the little church hall where the reception's going to be.

His family are all sat down on the left side of the room and the small amount of my family sat on the other side and none of them talking to each other; the divide in the room petrifies me. How do I turn this one and spin it in the air without it smashing to the ground and shattering into a million pieces?

Neither of the families know each other, they have never met before.

We walk to the top of the room where a white tablecloth had been placed over two school dining tables for the wedding party.

My mum and sister are still looking miserable and I'm still feeling bewildered by the atmosphere in the room and wondering what's going on.

The band is all set up on stage and the singer is my

now brother-in-law. He's married to the bridegroom's sister.

There's a set of drums in the background and Freddie begins to sing and play his guitar to the song: 'Pretty Woman', Roy Orbison style.

You see, Freddie is also a look-alike Roy Orbison and can sing like him too.

He plays around the clubs and pubs in town.

So, we're now having the first dance and I'm thinking 'Pretty Woman', how lovely, that's me.

As the song ends my mother in law taps me on the shoulder and, laughing, she says, "He played that for me!"

Well, that brings me back down to earth with a mighty bang.

I decide that while I've got the chance I'll go speak to my mum.

"Hi Mom," I say as I put my arm around her.

But she shrugs me off and says, "Piss off!"

I'm so shocked. "Mom, what's wrong, what have I done??

She said, "Just get away from me."

Then, my dad comes across and thinks I've upset her and starts as well but then my now-husband comes across and says, "Don't speak to my wife like that!!!

I don't know what's going on but I'm really struggling to contain all this confusion and unhappiness and don't know what to do about it all.

So I move me and him out of the way, trying to

spin another plate and keep them all in the air.

My head is spinning with confusion and it's not much of a happy wedding day.

I decide to dance to the rock n roll song the band are now playing but I can't move in my wedding dress, so I decide to change into something I can dance in. In no time at all, I appear out of the ladies loo in a long black dress fit for a funeral.

But he doesn't want to dance.

He wants to walk up the road to the shop and buy a packet of mints.

I said, "No, I'm not walking up to the shop dressed like this!"

Then, his two aunties appear and pipe up and say, "Oh, our little so and so has been really poorly lately, can she have your wedding bouquet?"

What could I say, the little girl was standing there and he was still going on about the mints!

So, I'm saying no to him and blurted out yes to them and I'm feeling even more bothered and unhappy.

I can't remember whether we went for the mints; we must have because when I came back to the church hall everyone had gone and all had been cleaned away.

I said, what's happened, where is everyone, where's all the buffet food???

Oh well. He said, "We had the hall for the amount of time and had to clear away so everyone's gone."

The truth was; my dad and his mates had put some cans of beer underneath their table so then, his father decided the party was over and started clearing everything away into the boots of cars to be transported back to their house.

My head is still in a fog and can't think straight at all as everything seems to be spinning out of control.

Then I'm in my mother-in-law's living room, with all his aunties sat on the chairs and sofa; he's in the kitchen with his family and I go and sit on the floor underneath the window; looking and listening as I'm trying to get my head around what's going on.

Then suddenly, it hit me just like a thunderbolt had struck the very core of me.

I'm petrified, more afraid than I have ever been in my life; I wanted to run out the door and never stop running till I got home but it was too late.

I was in it now, and couldn't see any way out.

I was well and truly trapped and in amongst the muffled sounds in the living room, I heard his aunties laughing as they said to me, "This is it, this is what you've got now, this is going to be for the rest of your life".

I wanted to vomit but I was paralysed; not from alcohol but from fear. Why couldn't I move?

Why, couldn't I just get up and walk out the door. and just go home now?

The voice in my head was screaming, 'Let me go!'

I've done everything expected of me, played all my parts and now I just want to go home.

But I couldn't move, I felt paralysed, stuck in the moment and stuck to the floor.

Unable to move.

Unable to speak, I sat there frozen in my doomed silence.

Pennsylvania Hexes

by Joe Murray-Smith

Folklore artwork is something often taken for granted. Many people look no further than the styles, the effects, the brushstrokes, colours and materials. Its setting and the feelings aroused by its compositions and styles. Many often do not look to the history of a specific piece of art and its origins, the told folklore inspired and woven into its histories. What other hidden meanings could it represent? Other than the easy observations a layperson may reflect upon, not instilling the real power from a piece of art.

Although many believe that they are purely just decoration, the power of Hexes and the mystery of their uses expands past the academic and digresses into a realm of myth and mysticism and the supernatural. The chilling events happened near the village of Amish, Pennsylvania. A small ricketed town built in 1823, with a population of 84. The ancestors of the Amish people were said to be involved in a cult ritual based on their own folklore and magic. They held the belief that on certain nights of the year the spirits of a dreamworld walked the earth, much like those of ancient communities of the past may have believed. The Amish often displayed around their village and surrounding forest a number of Hexes and had created a calendar that refers to the dates the spirits could be free and walk the earth and interact with the living. This is a written event of history proving that this folklore is true.

23rd November 1921. A stranger travelling the rural towns of America, researching the folklore of community village groups is restless, approaching the village of Amish the last light of day was fading, only the moonlight slowly awakening in the sky above to guide his steps through the Silver Forest in the twilight, it was named the Silver Forest for it's populous of silver birch trees, said to have magical properties that balance our two worlds. Earth and their dream world. The Amish believed that the bright birch trees shining silver bark gave off a glowing light that beams into the dreamworld and provides a barrier between the two spheres. This light separates the two and resolves the spirit's hunger for what the earth offers them and brings them peace taking away their insatiable lust to inhabit the earth. They had been known to take the life of the villagers or wanderers that happenstance to be there without this ritual barrier defending them.

Through this dense populous our stranger treaded, noticing hexes engraved into many of the birches painted white and purple and thickly carved into the birch tree. The stranger stopped at one in a clearing, where the light of the moon illuminated the pattern. He paused and eagerly consulted his notebook. Noticing the surrounding border of the hex a coronal reef of lavender, and in the centre, a silver birch image etched deeply and roughly into the tree. The stranger reflected on this, he jotted the symbol with the luminescence of the sky cast over him for light to draw in his notebook. He knew he must be getting closer to Amish village itself as the symbols are a certain sign of a cultist community nearby

He was reflecting on this fascinating folklore depicted in the company of the forest, as a sound in the blackness startled him. Crunch... crunch, crunch, crunch. He jerks his head anxiously, spinning and turning quickly on his feet but could not figure where the sound was coming from. It seemed it was from every fathom of the dark forest, wherever he turned he heard the same sound. Crunch.... crunch, crunch crunch, starting around him in the blackness. He stares into the penetrating jet black, fearful, he is frozen to the spot with a feeling of waking terror and hostility rising from his feet insidiously up his legs and spine to the back and the crown of his head like cold sharp needles over his body. where there was once intrigue is now a deathly mortal chill confirming deep in his nerves, a terrible sense for his survival fading within him, any control of fear he once had diminishing and disappearing. His hope lessening. He senses something in the darkness staring back though he cannot see it, just a sense he cannot resolve, his body so enveloped by the overpowering feeling of being eyed from the deepening chasms of the forest, Crunch.... crunch, crunch sounds again. Louder and closer this time.

A murmuring chant starts to develop residing deep in the darkness "Armar yan mar seute" is murmured in a sinister and resolute voice and one after the other, crunch.... crunch, crunch, crunch. Against all good intentions and will he trembles with fear. He anxiously turns to hear where the chant is residing but as with the footsteps, it seems to fathom from all around him. Before he even has time to reason his body suddenly flights in terror and haste and instinct he runs, staggering into the darkness with no sense of direction only a flawed instinct guiding him. He looks for light, the mortal sense that light will guide him safely and believing this, but unknowingly of this perceived churchdom he runs, trips and staggers through the forest, his breath quickening and deep like icicles stabbing from inside his heavy heaving chest, he gasps as they build and stab again, his chest heaves again with terror, stabbing and cutting within his chest, each breath so cold and tense he felt he could inhale no air. His throat clenching tight from the icy clammy dark

He runs, scrambling through the instilling darkness, past the trees, past silver birch, once again he sees the Hexes etched, illuminated in the moons certain glowing beams. Then another and another, he follows in hope of finding any relief from his heaving fear, his desperate search of hope and rescue and return to safety and reward and redemption. He desperately staggers with no bearing or clue of which way he was heading or where his staggered desolate footsteps are leading. The stranger struggles on, he notices a glowing, flickering amber light surrounded in the blackness ahead. He stumbles on toward it screaming from his icy stabbing chest "Hello!, hello, help! Save my soul!". He staggers closer to the glowing beam, his eyes squint and adjust in the cold dark with the light of the moon guiding his vision. He approaches, he hears more chanting and wailing

"Amar yan mar Suete, Amar yan mar Suete!" chanting and shrieks and wails thrive out from around amber flickers leaving him panic-stricken and a mortal chill once again rises up, and unrelenting terror chasms over his whole body. He turns round to the forest in flight and the same Crunch.... crunch, crunch, crunch and the same chant, "Amar yan mar Suete". Environed, surrounded and with no other direction to go he hurtles back toward the amber light. The closer he gets he sees brighter amber red flames dancing and twisting their way out of the darkness igniting in him a waking nightmare. The fire invoked more fear within him than before, but he instinctively ran toward it, the natural sense of terror in him responded once again. Following his own feet, running from the rising fear of death quick to overcome his pitiless hopes for salvation. He makes out silhouettes around the dancing, flickering fire blazing and a clammy moonlit horror now mirroring in his eyes. He freezes again overwhelmed with the threatful fear of death and hopelessness. He hears once again "Amar yan mar suete". The figures from the woods now appearing from its intangible black. They step out into a clearing. Dressed in devilish horned black masks with shredded linen covering their bodies from their head to the forest floor. All with arms clasped behind their back but frozen still like statues, then they take another step. With each step they chant, "Amar yan mar suete, Amar yan mar Suete," then freeze still. Then another step: "Amar yar man suete," they chant, they step forward forming a ring around him. The stranger cries filled with ceaseless fear the burning terror rising within him. The figures step out from the darkness. He is surrounded. "Amar yan mar Suete," they step closer, they encircle him. Thriving, chanting and shrieks instilling more terror upon him from the fatal black. They approach him residing out of the malignant black, the chant echoes creating a fatal pulse rippling through his mind, body and spirit. They lift him from the ground above their heads he screams and wails pitilessly with no respite. They strip him bare of clothes, he bellows with desperate shrieks and wails a hopeless plea for a blessed freedom, his desperation sinks deep, he shouts to god to save him from heinous terror. Writhing and terrified, his desperation diminishing, the mystic dark silhouetted figures thriving from his hopelessness of spirit and life. They hold him down, he cannot tear free.

From a badly formed pot of mud filled with blood, they paint the symbol of the silver birch on his chest with the ring of lavender surrounding. He screams one last time as they force the rest down his throat between cries and howls and malignant gurgles. Suddenly the pitiless screaming stops to a whimper, he falls silent, he goes completely lifeless as if life and spirit had left his body in one fatal moment. The chanting and shrieks around him subside to low murmurs and the circling figures step back in a slow ordered pace. All that is heard now is the crackling flames of amber fire and slow, fearful, murmuring of the mystic chant: "Amar yan mar suete." The figures step back again malignant and slow, life rises in the stranger once more, his chest now rising and falling not heavy but composed of steady resolute breaths. He starts to murmur within the figures around him, imitating their rhythm. "Amar yan mar Suete, Amar yan mar Suete," he repeats in a deep steady tone, building louder with insidious force the same chant repeated over again. Crookedly he rises to his feet contortedly and deformed, and hesitantly opens his eyes wide like two burning suns dancing and mirroring in the flames of the fateful fire.

A figure walks up to him and places the devilish mask over his head, trails the torn linen from head to toe and steps back. The figures chant. Instinctively he steps back from the centre and joins the ritual ring. "Amar yan mar Suete, Amar yan mar Suete," the fire kindles and flickers out, the circle disappears back to the far dark deviated company of the forest, the stranger with them, only the deep freezing night is left and the forest won't of life as if never inhabited in its desolation. Dulcet songs of birds are silent and void as if they never had residence in the black. Creatures of the forest are silent and still if any inhabit at all. The stranger disappears. He never makes it to the village of Amish.

Addendum:

The stranger was victim to the dream world. He had happened upon a ritual. The hexes carved into the silver birch were an invitation for the spirits to walk the earth from their dwellings in between our world and our universe, a place in-between both our earthly sphere and the outer celestial sphere of the universe. The hex was the key to the gateway, the silver birch tree represented the light that balances our two worlds, the coronal wreath of lavender represents the dimming of the light allowing the dreamworld spirits access through a gateway to inhabit our world and possess the stranger's body. The blood that was smeared over him and forced to drink was a lubricant for the spirit to possess his soul and take him deep into the forest and through to the celestial sphere of their dreamworld never to be human again. The headdress was a carved depiction of the spirits true likeness with the torn linen representing the silver birch tree, the white-silver bark that flickers shone by the moonlight. The words chanted 'Amar yan mar Suete'. 'Through the darkness and into the light,' the spirits chant to inhabit their earthly form.

Despite the stranger's eager interests, he fell victim to his misguided intrigue. His mistaken ignorance of the powerful hexes had led him into a terrifying ritual that possessed his body, his own curiosity guiding force of his damnation. Maybe some things are better to be left untouched, some things are too powerful for mortal minds and the secret art of metaphysics that conflicts with our delicate human nature. A deep respect for the justices of magic leads to a safer bright life away from the insidious dark and offering a balance of both celestial spheres to one's advantage and mortal humankind.

The Reclaimed

by Minnie Lansell

[Warning: some readers might find the theme of this story disturbing – Ed.]

A drop in the ocean

The sunlight lay in bright stripes across the hotel room as Claire pondered on the next paragraph of her latest article. She wanted to capture interest in the current rise of mental illness which was escalating, and Chile was designated as ground zero. She sucked on her pen as she pondered the facts laid out on the bed before her. Her husband, Frank, was shut in the bathroom developing photos he had taken of patients in the local school-turned-hospital. Their 11-month-old daughter was sleeping soundly in her cot. They were a husband-and-wife independent journalism team. Claire wrote articles for several large media outlets as well as her own blogs, while Frank provided stunning visuals to complement the stories. They spent their lives traveling the world for their next juicy lead. This time, they knew they were at the epicentre of a global pandemic and it was both terrifying and thrilling. When they had first heard about the sudden illnesses they decided to investigate and document the unfolding events. It was also a chance to visit Chile and enjoy some relaxation as a family. They had not anticipated the rapid severity of the situation. With such a young child they regretted their decision the moment they arrived. During the four-hour flight things had escalated from a health crisis to sheer panic and public discord. All outbound flights were either booked up or grounded.

Claire surveyed the collection of information and evidence they had collated over the last three days. The first incidents were noted in Chile and Argentina, spreading across the continent. Southern Africa and New Zealand were also hit hard. All borders were closed with immediate effect. Now, at day five, every country in the southern hemisphere had exponential increases of patients exhibiting symptoms of extreme psychotic violence and rabies.

Frank emerged from the bathroom in mid conversation on his phone.

"Yes, we can come down straight away. Meet you by the pool. I'm a redhead, beard and blue shirt. Claire has light brown curly hair and she's wearing a red top and cropped jeans. Green. Okay, see you shortly. Thank you. Bye."

He hung up excitedly. "I might have just got us a great lead, but we need to go now. Grab all that quickly."

"What lead?" she asked, gathering up the pages and photos then hastily slid them into a folder. "Is it from your conversation with that doctor yesterday?"

"Yeah, it's better than expected," he said, pulling a mask over Genevieve's face as she resettled herself in the baby carrier on his chest and went back to sleep. They headed down the short hall towards the stairs, both wearing masks.

"A pair of scientists have been studying the developments with a working theory. Anyway, they heard about our investigations and have been searching hotels for us all day. They want to compare notes." He held the door to the patio open for her. "I think we should see what they have to say and maybe help each other."

Claire nodded. There were a number of tourists sitting by the pool, in family groups. Nobody was really interacting outside their own circle.

"Gosh it's like Covid 19 all over again," a woman was saying to her teenage son. "I hope they don't close the pubs for another year!"

Claire rolled her eyes. "Now there's priorities for you," she said. "Oh look, those two women are waving at us!"

Frank smiled under his mask. One of the ladies was waving a green scarf just as she had said she would. The pair joined and exchanged greetings. Raised voices rang out behind them as two men yelled at each other and both lashed out at the woman trying to play peacemaker. Frank had barely moved his hand to undo the baby carrier when the taller scientist grasped his arm and shook her head.

"Don't," she said, in a low warning voice. "Probably infected." She nodded towards the rear exit which led to the beach, and they all walked away in silence. The sounds of an escalating brawl carried after them.

The sight which met their eyes left them all dumbfounded. There were fish everywhere. Not just fish but seals, dolphins, rays and sharks laid on the sand. Some dead, others writhing and flapping violently. An unspoken decision not to investigate moved them on.

They followed the path for a few minutes to an empty restaurant terrace overlooking the water. Both scientists removed their masks and indicated Claire and Frank do the same.

"It's safe," said the taller of the pair through a forced half smile. "We have a good idea what's happening and masks won't do anything. We just wore them because people will take us more seriously if we do."

Claire chanced a sceptical look at Frank who raised his eyebrows.

"First things first," said the slightly taller woman. "I'm Dr. Sofia Morgan, Infectious Diseases Physician and this is Dr. Annika Morgan, Climatologist and Meteorologist."

"We are Claire and Frank Jones. Investigative journalists."

Annika nodded. "Dr. Mendez told us you were asking to interview anyone with substantial information. Well, we have some answers and you have the media platforms to tell the world and save lives."

Sofia nodded and continued, "The local authorities are no use, there's too much happening and they're falling ill themselves."

"Yes," said Annika, "and the government are too concerned with taking credit themselves to really take us seriously."

Both women frowned. Frank was struck by how similar they were. Same dark hair and dark features. Both olive skinned with freckles. The way they finished off each other's sentences was almost comical, though they were quite serious. The main difference was that Sofia was taller and slightly slimmer than Annika. Clearly sisters.

Claire opened her folder and pulled out her wad of research. Soon everything was spread out and pinned down under glasses from the abandoned tables. "This is what we have," Claire said, feeling a bit simple in the company of such brilliant women of science.

Sofia examined the photographs of the infected, while Annika pawed at the maps which were marked with dates, times and estimated numbers of infections. She looked excited, which seemed rather inappropriate given the grim state of affairs.

"This is it," said Annika in triumph. "It all fits. Oh, this is terrible. It's …"

"What's going on then?" interrupted Frank. The pair re-seated themselves and paused. Claire whipped a dictaphone from her bag and started recording.

"Our friend Sean is, was, based at the Halley Research Station," said Sofia. "They called for assistance seven days ago when five members of the team started getting ill. Hallucinations, violent outbursts, delusions and sudden and extreme aquaphobia and anemophobia."

Frank looked puzzled.

"A fear of water and a fear of wind," she clarified.

He raised his eyebrows. "Rabies?"

"Yes, exactly. You've been doing your research." Sofia smiled but Claire was glaring and shook her head. She had told him about this that morning.

Sneaky git.

"Well anyway," continued Annika, "turns out several research stations were having the same outbreaks. Within hours every inhabited domain on Antarctica was under quarantine."

Claire put her finger on the world map. Antarctica was a central point of all currently infected countries.

"My God, it's spreading out from there! But how?" The answer hit her brain at the exact moment Sofia spoke.

"It's waterborne."

The rhythmic roar of the ocean now sounded sinister and threatening. Claire shuddered. She didn't know what to ask first.

Annika and Sofia nodded together.

"There's a parasite called Toxoplasma Gondii. T.Gondii for short. It's believed to be present in a third of Earth's population. It can remain dormant for years, but when it strikes it causes symptoms of psychosis and violence." Sofia paused for reaction. "It's quite remarkable, infected rats become suicidal and mental illness saw a huge increase in the early 1900s when feline domestication became popular."

"Because it's transmitted through cat poop," interjected Annika.

Claire had never felt so sick. Frank laid his hand on Genevieve's back and took slow deliberate breaths. His breakfast was seriously considering a reappearance.

Claire spoke in a whisper as if speaking aloud might make it more real. "But, rabies? Didn't you agree it was rabies?"

Sofia leaned in. "This is the fascinating thing. We have seen the original reports--"

"--Sean sent us copies."

"Yes, yes, and the blood samples showed a mutated version of lyssavirus."

"Rabies."

"And T. Gondii."

"Like an antigenic shift."

"That means they mutated together and evolved, probably over a million years in the frozen carcass of a dead mammal," said Sofia.

"Mmm, yes, there's been several large glacial ruptures lately. The contaminated ice melts, infects sea life and multiplies," continued Annika. "Non mammals can still carry these parasites. When did you last eat fish?"

Claire sat with her mouth open. Words were failing her.

Sofia waved her hand dismissively. "Annika, did you not see the beach? I would surmise that those creatures are indeed infected and self-sacrificed to spread the infection. Truly remarkable, really."

Claire swallowed hard. "So, you're saying that this Gandhi parasite has caught rabies and now it's swimming around infecting people? It's in the clam chowder?"

This was too much. Frank practically threw Genevieve at Annika and buckled sideways, vomiting all over the floor. Gen cried in surprise. Annika soothed her while Claire saw to Frank.

"I'll get you some water," she said automatically.

"NO!" Sofia was on their feet and walked off

swiftly into the restaurant leaving Annika to explain.

"It's waterborne! Tap water is no longer safe. Only drink from pre-packaged fluids. No swimming. No bathing. No seafood. Anything that involves unpackaged water in any way is a death sentence!"

"All these people are going to die?" gasped Claire, as the sudden realisation hit her hard. Annika stroked Gen's delicate red hair as if she was the most precious thing in the world.

"The last we heard from Sean, he had started with symptoms, and there were only two others still alive. The rest had either ripped each other apart or headed outside without protection. Infected or not, humans don't last very long against the wilds of Antarctica. Poor Sean was planning to eat a bullet sometime last night." She looked solemn and kissed the top of Gen's head. Frank sat down and took a bottle of water from Sofia who had returned with a box full.

"These are dated from over a month ago so should be safe," she said. "Fill your bags."

Annika stood and handed Gen to Claire. "Such a sweet thing. What's her name?"

"Genevieve," said Claire, smiling at her daughter. "The heat isn't agreeing with her. She's never slept so much."

Everyone looked at the little girl. She looked grumpy. Her green eyes were red from the heat and she pouted as she wound her fingers into her mother's hair. No words were exchanged but, in that moment, they knew that she was the future. The children needed a chance, and they were the best ones to provide it.

Pandemonium

The video was rough. Frank filmed Claire interviewing Sofia and Annika, highlighting the facts and urging governments to act.

As they returned to the hotel, they stopped briefly to capture footage. Some infected were now fighting on the beach. None were entering the water, but their rages seem to have accelerated past the aquaphobia. Annika pointed a little way out to sea at something big moving closer at speed. They remained rooted to the spot as a large, dark blue whale broke the waves and beached itself upon the sand, clamping its gigantic jaw shut upon two infected fish. Frank almost dropped the camera in disbelief.

The sun was beginning to sink and the air was cooling. Human remains floating in the pool confirmed the outcome of the brawl and the building was eerily quiet.

Twenty minutes of speedy editing and the video was uploaded and emailed to every news and scientific source they could think of. Thank goodness the wi-fi still worked!

"What do we do now?" asked Sofia. For the first time she sounded helpless. She must have heard it herself because she added, "Our focus has been on getting the information out, but we never gave much thought past that point."

"We should stick together," said Frank. "We can watch out for each other and find a way out."

Silence.

At least an hour passed before the phone started to ring. Claire spoke in disbelief for a few minutes, mostly saying, "yes" and then, "Chile Chico at ten. Got it." She hung up. Everyone waited with bated breath.

"That was a General from a base somewhere in the US. He said he couldn't disclose his location further but our video has changed everything. He said it's saving lives and they want us to go there." She put her hand on her forehead and took a shaky breath. "An extraction team will be at Chile Chico Airport at 10pm today. We've to get there."

Sofia was quickest. "I've got it on Google maps. We need a car?" In a quick discussion they decided to pack some essentials and head straight to the airport.

Out in the street there was chaos. The flaking white painted buildings were splattered with bullet holes and blood. It was difficult to know who might be infected and who was simply rioting. They kept to the walls where possible. Annika clutched Gen against her in the carrier while Frank took the lead, a piece of railing in hand, and Claire took the rear wielding a broken chair leg. They made good time and had almost reached the edge of town by dark. Street lights illuminated shadows moving up and down the road.

Suddenly, an angry screech split the night. A man in ripped, bloody clothes stood on the bonnet of a car. He looked menacing. His breathing was rapid and heavy. In the dim light his eyes looked blood shot and he was foaming at the mouth. Jumping down, he sprinted at them, hands raised ready to strike. Someone else was running right behind him. Frank swung his pole hard and it connected with the side of the man's head. At the exact same moment, the second man had swung a crowbar from the other side and there was a clink as the metals connected in the centre of the now pulverised skull. Brain matter splattered the ground and the arm of Frank's jacket. Frank automatically raised his weapon again, but the man raised a hand and backed away.

"Gracias!" called Claire, and she urged them forwards.

They paused two streets away to catch their breaths. It was deserted but the dark night was filled with distant screams, alarms and gun fire. Frank bent double and vomited the sparse remains of his stomach onto the pavement. Sofia promptly joined him and a second later Annika made it a hattrick. Claire, meanwhile, was examining cars. She pulled a first aid kit and a flash light from a crashed van and headed to a truck a little way up the road. The keys were in the ignition! She climbed in and started the engine. It spluttered to life.

"Over here. Quickly!"

The group piled into the truck. Sofia and Frank sat in the open back. They passed crashed cars and infected people. Some chased the truck. Others went under the wheels, causing the passengers to be tossed about. The airport was lit up like a belisha beacon. They made a cautious entrance into the small seemingly empty building. There was blood smeared across the floor and bullet holes in the walls.

Claire gripped Frank's hand. They crossed to the door out to the runways but a high-pitched cry made them all leap out of their skins. Genevieve had now had enough: she wailed loudly and Annika had no luck calming her. Claire lifted her daughter out of the carrier and cuddled her.

"She must be starving; she hasn't eaten in hours," she said checking her watch. She sat down and unbuttoned her top. Genevieve fed hungrily while the others checked for food. They all jumped again at the sound of knocking on glass. A security guard looked back at them. He held up his hands to show he meant no harm. Frank waved him towards them. The guard walked through the door carrying a grey looking girl, about ten years old.

"Mi hija, Esmeralda." He looked down at her as tears fell. She looked traumatized. A bloody bandage was wrapped around her left arm.

Frank pointed to the girl's arm and then slowly unwrapped the bandage. A chunk of flesh had been bitten away.

Anika helped clean and redress the wound. Frank kept hold of his pole just in case.

With basic Spanish, they were able to surmise that Esmeralda's mother had become unwell after a day at the beach. Alejandro arrived home to find his wife missing and Esmeralda bitten. When he got back to the airport all the pilots were gone.

"US army," said Annika kindly. She looked at the others. "Surely they will have room?"

Claire shrugged. Genevieve became livelier in the cool night air. Soon the rumbling sound of a plane gradually grew closer. It was a hard landing. Three armed soldiers descended and made their way towards the rag tag group.

"Who are the extra two?" demanded the Captain.

"An airport guard and his daughter," said Frank. "Listen, the girl's--"

"Essential to ongoing research and we need her," Sofia said sternly.

The captain eyed Esmeralda's arm and frowned. "Reeker?" he said. "As in *reclaimed*," he added, tapping his head.

Sofia spoke in hushed tones, "She's bitten, yes. That's why I need her. This is as close to patient zero as I'm going to get, and she might hold the key to saving humanity. Restrain her if you're worried, but she *has* to come."

The captain sighed. "Restrain the girl."

Twenty minutes later they were refuelled and airborne in a cargo plane heading to an airbase in Los Angeles.

"Did you say that just to try and save her, or do you really want to cut her up for science?" asked Claire, unsure of Sofia's motives.

"Both," said Sofia staring ahead.

Claire looked away.

"Don't forget, what happens between now and the end of the world has the potential to prevent the latter," Sofia said. "And make no mistake. We are a hair's breadth from the end."

Claire held Genevieve close to her.

"I'll make every conceivable effort to save the girl," said Sofia in a genuine tone. "I'm not Dr

Frankenstein."

The End of Days

The eleven-hour flight was nearing its end, and everyone was dozing side by side. Esmeralda had been sedated and restrained towards the front of the aircraft but was now stirring and struggling against her bonds. Alejandro clutched a rosary while lovingly stroking his daughter's hair. She stared up at him through angry bloodshot eyes. As he bent over her and kissed her on the forehead he stiffened, thrashed his arms about then fell silently to the floor. A gaping hole had been bitten in his throat. Esmeralda snapped her bindings with unbelievable strength and launched herself at the sleeping airmen. Her little fingers jabbed into eye sockets, tearing flesh and spraying the walls with blood. Her teeth sank into the second airman's throat. She ripped his larynx apart to the sound of the first airman drowning in his own blood upon the floor.

The sound of shots jolted the group awake. Gen was screaming, Annika began hyperventilating and Sofia looked stricken and disorientated. The plane was tipping into a nose-dive. Equipment swung forward in its restraints as Frank looked around in helplessness. Shouts from the cockpit signalled someone was still alive. He slid down the plane clinging to anything he could, skating through the bloodbath of bodies, to the single surviving airman attempting to regain control of the aircraft. Esmeralda's grey corpse was draped limply over the second pilot. Bullet holes in both of them matched the holes in the instruments and windshield.

"We're going down," screamed the pilot. "Radio is shot!"

"What can I do?" shouted Frank.

"Pray."

The plane levelled out slightly, but they were still in descent. Frank screamed, "Emergency landing!" back down the walkway and dived for a seatbelt. The plane bounced hard on impact and tilted sideways. A penetrating grind of metal on road threatened to explode the fuel tanks like the reaper rolling a dice.

When they came to a standstill, Gen was hysterical. Sofia moaned and sat up holding her left arm. Annika whimpered as they detangled themselves from the fallen supplies and slowly dragged each other forwards.

Frank was helping the semi-conscious pilot.

They were on a country lane surrounded by fields. Claire and Frank quickly ejected the dead onto the road and resecured the door. Just in case.

"It feels so disrespectful," sobbed Annika while setting a sling around Sofia's visibly broken arm. "I'm so frightened."

Claire pushed Gen into her lap. "She likes you," she said. "You're really good with kids."

Sofia gave Claire an appreciative nod.

Frank reappeared looking grave. "The lad's alive, but he's bitten." His words sounded forced and weighted. "He's only nineteen."

Sofia's voice cracked. "This is my fault."

The silence was suffocating. The pilot, Ben,

assisted Frank in patching the radio enough to get coordinates back to base. Help was inbound when reality inevitably hit. Ben snarled and kicked as he tried to resist the reclaiming. Time had run out.

Frank stepped up. Raising the boy's own gun, he silenced his rage.

It was a sombre party that watched the lights of two armoured trucks approach later that night. The five held hands and vowed to remain together as they faced the end of days.

The Honour of a Thief

by Junior Mark Cryle

Night time at the house, lights are out, the owners asleep, not a peep except for the sound of glass-cutting.

A square popped from the window but was stopped before hitting the ground by a well-placed suction cup, held by a being hidden by the shadows around him.

Getting into the house? Easy. Getting out? A doddle.

Getting what he came for without waking anyone? That's the challenge.

Luckily he was not alone, thanks to modern technology.

"Call: Pointdexter," he whispered into his Bluetooth headset. One 'ping' later, he was connected. "I'm in. What's your status?"

"A door away from bailing when things go south, all because my suggestion of getting this from eBay was shot down," a voice replied. "Again."

"I meant on the alarms."

"Oh, yeah, the window's clear, working on the rest. I'm just saying this is a bit too far."

"All's fair in love and war," he replied as he scouted the ornaments.

"But to steal from your girlfriend's parents?" the voice asked.

"If they cared, they would've given it to her by now."

"Given how rare this is, wouldn't she put two and two together?"

"She hasn't left me yet."

"Doesn't mean she's okay with it. I mean, is this really worth the risk?"

"I believe that 'actions speak louder than words,' my friend. As long as what I bring can make her feel happy and loved, even for a moment," - he spied the objective that he sought - "then I'll make sure her family pays for it, every time."

He held the item, then slowly placed it inside his bag with the greatest of care.

"Am I good to go?"

"I've taken care of all the alarms, as you asked—"

BEEP! BEEP! BEEP! BEEP!

"-- Except for the front door. Well, good luck with that. Bye." CLICK!

Without missing a beat, he dashed through the door and towards freedom, all while cursing modern technology between breaths.

He felt it strange that, as he ran across the garden, there wasn't any security to slow him down. No guards or--

"Freeze!" yelled a guard.

Three guards total, in hot pursuit. Two of them scattered left and right in a pincer movement, evidently confident in their fitness to attempt the manoeuvre.

What they didn't bank on, however, was that the thief majored at gymnastics in his spare time, so as he grabbed a bamboo stick from a lone potted plant and used it to pole-vault over the garden wall effortlessly, they were helpless as their efforts earned them some quality time with said wall.

As the thief fled, stick still in hand, he made a mental note to bring his gymnastic equipment on heists more often. Across the streets he silently approached a rather plain bungalow, a pocket-born key at hand proved it was his residence.

A job well done, he quietly opened the door, closed and locked it behind him, then made his way towards the living room.

A bright light blinded him without warning, he recognised that someone switched the lamp on, someone who wasn't him.

"What did you do?" spoke the one beside the lamp. Her dressing gown and tied-up hair meant that she had been waiting for him. How long? Irrelevant. She was mad, which meant he was in trouble.

"And good evening to you too, dear," he said. "You didn't have to wait up for—"

"--What. Did. You. Do?"

"Would you believe I was in the shower?"

"Outside, on a summer night, in your work gear?"

"That's a no, then. I was hiking?"

"Believable, with you having a stick-on hand. But not so much if you recall that the surrounding countryside areas are all privately owned. No public access."

'So close,' he thought. Before he gave up.

"I had a last-minute job to do. A small one, nothing went wrong."

Her glare hit him, the one thing he feared.

"Well, there was an alarm and a guard," he corrected.

Still she glared.

"Okay, three guards," he admitted. "But all taken care of. Honestly, I'd thought your family had better security for—"

"--You stole from my family?"

If he had false legs, he'd put them in his mouth. Feet first. "In my defence—"

"--What defence? They're my family!" she yelled. "They may not have respect for me anymore, but I thought you had enough respect to not steal from them. What possible reason could you have to risk legal action by doing this?"

"See for yourself," he replied.

As he'd hoped, her furious gaze vanished, replaced with surprise at the revealed item: a porcelain doll, one that she recognised as her grandmother's. They'd played with it often when she visited as a child. It had become hers on her thirteenth birthday, a year before her grandmother passed away.

The doll, along with the rest of her cherished possessions, was denied to her when the family disowned her, when she made her relationship with a commoner known to them, therefore claimed the items as family heirlooms. She resigned herself to the fact that she would never see her childhood treasures again.

Yet there it was.

As her tears fell, she held the doll as tightly as she dared, partly in fear that it'd disappear if she didn't. Memories, of smiles and laughter that she thought forgotten, returned eagerly.

She then embraced the man who brought her such joy.

The man who made his career known at her insistence within their first year together.

The man who stole not for fame or fortune, but to return what was once hers.

The man she loved dearly, and who loved her enough to perform such deeds.

"How did you know?"

"Our last date," he answered. "You clearly missed it and I, a good Samaritan, thought I'd return it to you. Plus, your birthday was coming up this weekend and, well, two birds and all that." He heard a giggle from her, then he asked, "So, am I still in trouble?"

"Given the circumstances," she slowly said, "I believe a reward and a punishment are in order. For such a thoughtful gift, you shall not be sleeping on the sofa."

That made him smile, before she continued.

"But since you stole it, I believe being denied your picks for this month's movie nights should be enough. And guess what? Tomorrow's movie night, and I'm dying to check out this rom-com musical with you." With a good night kiss, she went to bed.

Once alone, he slumped on the sofa, defeated.

While the couple generally got along, their tastes

in films were like sugar and salt, sweet when it’s his choice, salty when it's not.

“In hindsight,” he thought aloud, “maybe I was better off being caught.”

We Are The Gordons!

by Caroline Stockwell-Brown

Mr and Mrs Gordon are an ordinary couple. They had been married for over forty years. Edith was a bubbly, vivacious, friendly lady always ready for a chat and to give any activity a go. James was a quieter fellow, happy to be by himself on his iPad, strumming his guitar or enjoying quiet solitary fishing.

Lockdown had been a mixed blessing for them. During the first lockdown they had made a list of all those little jobs that needed attention (well, Edith had). Within a few weeks everywhere in their house and garden was spick and span and they were really pleased with themselves. For a few days Edith and James sat in their garden and enjoyed looking at their successful work. However, the lockdown didn't end to their timetable and as the weeks went by they got quite fed up (well, Edith did).

They did make the most of their hour's exercise allowance each day and cycled around their neighbourhood, revelling on the quiet roads, enjoying the glorious weather during the enforced home stay.

Edith was particularly disappointed that she was not able to see her grandchildren, who only lived around the corner. But no, their son was adamant they all had to stay at home. He had even put the car in the garage and locked the gates up to the drive, so they would all stay in their little cocoon.

When the summer finally came, Edith immediately booked a little cottage in the Peak

District. It had been quite a search, as of course everyone was doing the same. The pandemic meant that flying abroad was not recommended and flights were often cancelled.

The Peak District did not live up to Edith's hopes. There was no hot tub and only an open fire to warm the cottage which took more effort than Edith had remembered as a child. Then there were no nearby pubs or restaurants, so Edith had to do all the cooking. It was not how she wanted a holiday to be at all.

So, Edith came home a bit fed up and immediately tried to book another little break but everywhere was so booked up. Then her son caught the dreaded Coronavirus. He hadn't realised it at first and he was lucky it was only a mild dose. There was much debate about how he became infected and there was general agreement that a week's holiday in their caravan was the cause. Fortunately, neither his wife or children caught it, which remained a mystery to Edith, as she so often said. After all, they were all living together and no-one had yet been vaccinated.

Her son did now relent a bit and let the grandchildren visit their grandparents. But they had to stay in the garden and keep two metres apart! No cuddles, cried Edith, not happy at all. But at least she could entertain her grandchildren with games and crafts and baking and for a while she was very happy. She wasn't so sure when she was given some home schooling to do with them! It was all new to her and getting onto the right lesson on the computer was a problem in itself. This was unexpected as she had always considered herself up on these things when she had been working. But she did laugh when the teacher gave her a gold star for all her efforts!

Whilst it was lovely to see the grandkids, Edith still longed to go away. Everywhere was closing again with another virus spike. The lessons stopped and Edith and James were locked in again. The cold weather came which curtailed the cycling and any gardening. So Edith set about sorting the photos but it just made her yearn even more to go away. One evening, as she was complaining to James about this, he suggested that they borrow 'our lad's caravan'. Hmm, thought Edith. It was a big caravan and she wasn't sure their car was strong enough to pull it. She didn't fancy taking out such a big thing, even if her son would consider it. It was his pride and joy and wouldn't be happy if it came back with a scratch or two. But James' throwaway comment set her thinking and she began her internet search for smaller caravans. Then she saw a motorhome and that did look promising. But how to encourage James...

Then Edith hit upon an idea. Her Mum had had a campervan in her later years and so she began chatting to James about the funny stories her mother had told them. They were soon laughing at the tales and memories. Just at the right time Edith showed James a campervan for sale. It looked just like her Mum's. Without realising it James was hooked! He liked technology and how things worked and was interested in the mechanics of it all. They saw several possibilities, at prices they could afford. Now they were both hooked!

Edith and James had formed a social bubble with their friend Shirley. During her next visit Shirley learned, to her surprise, that Edith and James were off to Norfolk to buy a campervan. Edith couldn't wait to show her the pictures and talked about driving it to Scotland, even across to France to see her sister! One evening they even tried to fathom if it was possible to get to Australia to visit their other son and family but after several hours decided it was a step too far. All this when the world was in the middle of a pandemic!

Next time Shirley spoke to Edith she politely asked how the trip to Norfolk went.

"Oh" said Edith, "we ended up in Shropshire…"

Edith then went on to tell her about a campervan they had gone to look at but hadn't actually seen because her iPad kept bringing up all these other campervans for sale in Shropshire.

"It was as though they knew we were there," said Edith.

"Have you bought one?", asked a rather tentative Shirley.

"Oh yes," said Edith. "We couldn't actually drive it as it had no engine and was cramped in a corner covered in tarpaulin, bikes and wood. We've come home to sort the money and the chap is going to get it ready for us. A really friendly chap he was, been camping for years!"

Coming off the phone, Shirley was worried. But she knew Edith, once she had an idea there was no stopping her!

The next time Shirley visited her friends, she couldn't miss seeing the campervan parked in the front garden. To her relief it looked in good condition. James and Edith (well, mostly Edith) were full of information about their new van, even showing her the two full bags of instructions and service receipts they had been given.

The Gordons planned to try out the van that weekend at a small campsite about twenty miles away.

"Just to test it out," said Edith. "We will take the car too, just in case."

Fortunately all went well, although James and Edith drew up a list (well, mostly Edith) of 'little' things that needed doing. Over the next months, Edith shared with Shirley her plans to change the curtains, buy new pots and pans and respray the van (she thought it too dull). They wanted to fit a rear camera to help with parking and some racking to store their bicycles. Then there were the new lighter deckchairs and a new roof (the original having a leak) plus a hundred and one other 'little' additions.

Shirley quietly mused to herself whether all Edith's 'little' additions wouldn't end up costing more than the campervan itself!

Then came another Covid lockdown, so Edith and James (well, mainly Edith) had plenty of time to work through the list. It also gave them time to join every conceivable camping and caravanning club known to man!

The Gordons' house now became full of camping books, maps and mattresses, curtain material and other things Edith felt couldn't be left in the campervan. Shirley did wonder how on earth they'd fit it all in. But she just smiled and nodded as Edith told her of their plans once lockdown was over.

At last Edith and James were ready for their first real trip. They had decided on going to Norfolk, an area they were unfamiliar with. The journey was uneventful and when they arrived at the site it was a lovely woodland park much closer to Sandringham than they thought.

They set themselves up and hooked into the electricity.

Their first morning dawned bright and sunny, so they put out their chairs and table to enjoy breakfast 'Al Fresco'. Edith was making toast when a man came by and said:

"Good morning, lovely day."

"Yes," said James in a totally disinterested manner.

Quickly, Edith dashed out to chat, knowing that James wouldn't invite any more discussion.

"Hello," said Edith, in her friendly way. "It's such a lovely site here, do you visit often? It's our first time."

The gentleman smiled at Edith's enthusiasm.

"Yes, I've been a few times," he said. "Are you here on your own or have you a family with you?"

Edith proceeded to tell the chap all about her family and where they all lived.

He listened as politely as he could but to an outsider they would have noticed that his feet were shuffling. Eventually he seized the opportunity, when

Edith took a breath, to say:

"Oh, well it's lovely to meet you, Mr and Mrs Gordon but I have a full English waiting for me, so enjoy!"

With that, he turned and walked off.

Edith was quite disappointed to lose her chance to chat. But was also a bit flustered: the chap had used their name. She was about to raise this with James when he unexpectedly said, "Why haven't we got bacon and eggs?"

"What?" said Edith. "You've got toast and I brought your favourite type of marmalade especially. You know how bacon would smell out the whole van and linger for days. That's really annoying. I go to all this effort and you're still not satisfied. Now you've made me lose my train of thought."

Of course, when Edith was relaying the story to Shirley she hadn't mentioned all this but did repeat the conversation that followed. Edith said she was bemused that the man had known their names.

Edith and James (well, mostly Edith) had spent some time over their toast and coffee trying to figure out how the stranger had known who they were. At first they thought that he had read it in the site register. Or perhaps he was MI5 providing security for Sandringham and had come to check them out. There was talk that their phones were bugged.

"The worst of it," said Edith, "was that we didn't get to visit Sandringham because they were in mourning for Prince Philip."

The MI5 'surveillance' didn't dampen Edith's enthusiasm for camping and she had booked another week's break at Buxton.

Off they went again and parked up at a site just outside of the town. They spent happy days enjoying the countryside and shops (well, Edith did). One evening they had decided to treat themselves to a meal out, as the pubs and restaurants had finally reopened.

They found themselves a lovely old 16th century coaching inn, 'The Jug and Bottle'. They were sitting at the bar trying to decide between the scampi or the gammon, when a tall chap in casual clothes came in and greeted every person in the pub by name. He then approached Edith and James saying:

"Well, hello there, you must be the Gordons?"

He then purposely addressed James and said:

"Have you found our good local fishing spots?" Without waiting for an answer, he mentioned two places for good sport and had a conversation about tackle, rods and worms.

Edith stood there dumb founded. She hadn't seen James so eloquent in years and with a total stranger!

It was the next day when Edith asked James how he knew the angler from the pub. James said that was the first time they had met. There followed a heated discussion (well, mainly Edith) about how the man knew their names and James' love of fishing. It all ended in total silence when Edith, on cooking dinner, discovered James had used their only tin of sweetcorn for bait.

Their next trip was to Northumberland where they stayed near Alnwick. Edith loved books and couldn't wait to visit the amazing Station Bookshop nearby. With Covid still prevalent, the bookshop was empty, and Edith was able to browse the shelves at her leisure. James was enjoying a book about angling whilst sipping coffee.

An elderly gentleman entered the shop and was browsing nearby to Edith.

"Hello," said the man, being friendly. Edith was delighted and soon they were chatting away (well, Edith was) about the various merits of Joanne Trollope over Kate Atkinson. The man politely nodded but returned the books he had to the shelves and when Edith finally drew breath, he jumped in saying:

"I'm so sorry Mrs Gordon, I have to go. I'm on my bike and as you know, it takes time to get anywhere on two wheels, what with the hills hereabouts. But enjoy your holiday and bike rides." And with that, dashed out of the shop.

Edith finished her selection of books and she and James left to return to the campervan. Edith questioned James about the man at some length. But James was bemused not having noticed the person Edith was ranting about. Edith was not impressed!

Once again, back home Edith was telling her friend Shirley about their trips. Fortunately, Shirley was staying overnight so Edith had plenty of time to regale her with all the intricate details, including the one thing that she was still fretting about. Just how had these local men known they were the Gordons, that James fished and she cycled?

Edith had told her son, neighbours and friends on the phone but all had been politely bemused. Edith's theory about MI5 was explored or that maybe the campervan was being watched by police because it had been used before for people trafficking? Or maybe it was something to do with Covid? The mystery played on Edith's mind and she kept talking about it all weekend to Shirley.

Shirley was taking her leave and Edith went with her to the car, which Shirley had parked beside the campervan. Just before she left, Shirley pointed to the sticker they had put on the campervan window. It was a cartoon-like drawing with a man in fishing gear and a lady on a bicycle. Underneath were printed the words: "We are the Gordons".

Never had Shirley seen Edith lost for words and as she drove off saw Edith standing staring at the innocent sticker that had caused such commotion!

Village Lives

by Catherine Dean

From the start of the first lockdown in March 2020, I have been staying with my parents in a small village twenty miles to the north of York. Almost every day, my mother and I have gone on daily walks round the village and into the surrounding countryside. Whilst on our excursions we have met several local people, some known to my parents and others with whom they had had little contact previously. Each time we met the neighbours, some wanted to chat about their experiences, whilst others just said a cheery hello. I have selected a few of the neighbours to write about and give some idea of life during the past year's unprecedented time. I have changed the names of the people to protect their identities.

Bob and Hazel Thompson – Chapter 1 - 2020

On several occasions we have met Hazel and Bob Thompson on our daily constitutional walk, which we take come rain or shine. Hazel always tells us anecdotes about her life in the village. It has been a privilege to be able to talk to her during lockdown, although her news has not always been good. Hazel is a small lady in stature, with short greying hair and horn-rimmed spectacles. She is well-kempt and always wears a pretty dress.

On a few occasions early last summer we met Bob and Hazel sitting on a seat their son had put there, about a mile out of the village. Hazel had walked alongside Bob on his mobility scooter. We noticed then that his communication was poor, although he did offer us a beaming smile. We also saw him near to their cottage, using a walking frame as Hazel was keen that he had some exercise. He was prone to following her out into the garden when she was watering the plants. This worried Hazel as she was concerned that he might fall on the concrete path. Later, we saw them sitting on a bench closer to home, known to us as, 'Miss Bissett's Bench'. This seat had been the favourite of an old neighbour, who used to walk there to read her 'Cadfael' by Ellis Peters.

Bob has had some recent falls - probably caused by Parkinsons and the onset of early Dementia. At one point he expected his wife to help him off the floor, but this was impossible for a woman of her size. In the end a team of two or three family members had to lift him off the floor. Later, when he fell particularly badly, the paramedics had to be called. He was taken into hospital. Whilst there someone on the ward tested positive for Covid 19 so he had to be moved to a care home and isolated as a precaution. Once he had spent two weeks in the care home he returned home to Hazel. He went on to have several more falls. The cycle of emergency rescues by family and neighbours, from the village, kept repeating itself. Finally, he fell against the wardrobe door in the bedroom and broke the mirror, cutting his head in the process. Hazel described to us in graphic detail the wound on his head which, 'poured blood'. She was forced to leave him where he had fallen, whilst she telephoned for help. He was taken to hospital and later transferred to another care home to isolate once more. Sadly, he remains there as a care package to cater for his needs is taking a long time to put in place. It is a shame that Bob has lost his independence and further mobility whilst in the home.

Hazel and one of her two sons are only allowed a visit once a fortnight. The son, Peter, cried on one occasion as they were carefully supervised by staff. Hazel and her son sat at one end of a long table whilst Bob and his designated carer sat at the other. Peter, who is a policeman, said it was worse than prison. Bob has always been a stalwart of the village. The older villagers looked to him for guidance and advice.

He served for many years on the parish council, and ran tractor runs for the Yorkshire Air Ambulance and Marie Curie, this took him all over the country and on one occasion a friend of mine saw him on his beloved blue tractor in the centre of York. Every fortnight on a Saturday he and Hazel ran a bingo session in the village hall, where he also served on the committee. Having lived in this village for most of their lives, and both being born and working in villages not too far away, they have several relations who can be called upon to assist, but with Covid restrictions this can be difficult.

Last year, when times were normal, we were able to offer the couple pears from our tree as Bob is particularly fond of them. Hazel made us a delicious fruit cake as a thank you. Hazel is renowned for her baking and in times past had a small business run from her home, baking and icing cakes.

Bob and Hazel's house is a very small, thatched cottage with a large garden to the side and rear. The small front garden is always a mass of colour with beautiful fuchsias, begonias, geraniums and other flowering shrubs. The garden, at the side, is put to good use, growing a vast array of fruit and vegetables.

Bob is now home from the care home once more under Hazel's command. She had investigated getting a stair lift but the cost was prohibitive. A friend of hers commented, 'You should be able to get a stairway to the moon for that price!' Bob now sleeps downstairs, where their former dining room has been turned into a bedroom. Hazel was sad to part with her polished dining table. With limited help from carers, Hazel watches him carefully as he sits in the doorway on warmer days. He can release the brake on his wheelchair, and this could result in him being propelled down the two concrete steps. On one occasion she had asked a neighbour who was passing to keep an eye on him whilst she visited the bathroom. Fortunately, one of her sons has now fool-proofed the chair so it cannot move. On the odd occasion we do receive a warm smile or wave from Bob, but sadly his communication is very restricted, and it is not clear how much he can take in. Hazel always enjoys a quick word. Two weeks ago, we noticed a silver balloon outside the cottage. We noted it was to celebrate their Diamond Wedding - sixty years of marriage. Hazel was grateful for the belated card we sent to mark the occasion. Sadly, now that the weather has cooled the door to the cottage is usually closed, which must add to the feeling of isolation. It seems a pity that we are unable to go inside for a chat.

Chapter 2 - 2021

A few weeks ago, my father was told that Bob had taken a turn for the worse and it was therefore no surprise to discover two days later that he had died. It was a sad loss for the village as he had been known and respected by everyone. We read of the funeral arrangements in the local newspaper. Sadly because of Covid restrictions the usual funeral could not take place. In normal circumstances the numbers who would have attended the service would have been huge, necessitating relaying the service outside the church. As it was, only thirty mourners were allowed. The funeral time was given and an announcement made that the procession would leave the family home about twenty minutes before. The whole village turned out to line the route from Bob's house to the main road. The coffin was carried on a trailer, which was pulled by Bob's tractor and driven by his youngest son. The hearse carried floral tributes, one with blue flowers creating a tractor and further floral tributes in the form of a spaniel dog. This was a tribute to Bob's love of dogs during his working life as a farm labourer, and in particular to his son's two brown spaniels which Bob had enjoyed a special relationship with.

On several occasions recently when we have seen Hazel, she is accompanied by the two spaniels. She told us recently that the older dog is blind, but he is so familiar with her cottage that he can manage to navigate around. She said her sons wouldn't hear of him being put down because of his disability. The younger dog is more of a handful!

Last week she told us the story of her new coat. She needed one for the funeral and, being unable to go to the shops to choose one, her son had found a website for her to select a suitable garment. He showed her the selection on his smartphone. Being a sensible Yorkshire woman, she was adamant that she didn't want a black coat as she wouldn't wear it again; instead she chose one called 'Olive' as it had her name on it. At least, her middle name. Her son paid extra for delivery the following day in plenty of time for the funeral, just in case it didn't fit! There were ructions when it didn't arrive on the expected date, but her son rang her the next morning to say it would be delivered by twelve o'clock the following day - fortunately it did arrive and fitted her perfectly, so ensuring good use.

She talks about Bob often and told us that she was relieved that he had been with her right to the end. It seems that she can go out more now as we have seen her on more than one occasion being chauffeured by a younger family member. There have also been several people helping her with the garden, planting and rotavating. We saw her one day with a large rhododendron plant which had been a gift from the Air Ambulance on Bob's Ninetieth birthday. She was in the process of repotting it as she had found loads of weevils in its roots.

We look forward to the coming days of warmer weather when we can continue to see Hazel and the two spaniels and hear more stories.

Penny and Martin Thornton

On our daily walks in the village, we have met Penny several times. She lives in a terraced house, which is round the corner from my parents', with her husband, Martin. Penny and her husband also own the adjoining house, where their daughter is living temporarily, as she has been furloughed from her job in the Dales. Their son recently moved to America, where he now lives with his American wife in Florida. Penny and Martin have been to see them on two occasions, but Penny says she finds the heat too much, and she finds the air-conditioning gives her a headache.

Penny is a strong character. She can often be seen in her front garden or taking her terrier for a walk. The first occasion we met Penny once lockdown began, was on a Sunday. She was anxious to tell us that it was the first time in years when she hadn't had to cook Sunday lunch for over three hundred people. She usually works in a hotel on the moors where she is head chef. I imagine she is good at her job and efficient. She will not suffer fools gladly and can be direct when giving her opinions. I wouldn't like to get on the wrong side of her.

Not only does she work full time but she is also chair and secretary of the parish council, and in her spare time helps at the local stables with riding for the disabled. She also organises pony club events. Last week she told us of the problems with the children social distancing. The owner of the stables is now using a broom handle to show the children how far apart they need to be!

Penny's husband works for the local council maintenance team and can often be spotted working in the local villages. He is kept very busy during the cold weather in gritting the roads. He can get a call at three in the morning to head for the depot to collect salt. During lockdown we have seen him in Kirkbymoorside mending the paving stones and in our village filling in potholes. He is a cheery person and enjoys most of his free time on his allotment next to his house. His wife seems to marvel at the fact he can fall asleep as soon as he sits down in the evenings – I think it is hardly surprising!

One day last week, we walked up the road on our daily constitutional. As we rounded the bend at the corner, we spotted Penny just getting out of her car. She was carrying a home-made material mask in her hand. She greeted us with a beaming smile. "It is good to see you both again," she chortled.

Mum asked if she was back at work. "Back at last! I have been furloughed for one hundred days – I told my boss that I had enjoyed my retirement, picking fruit and veg from our allotment and doing my chores."

Penny told us what was happening at her workplace. "We are working at just over fifty percent capacity with tables distanced two metres apart and a booking only policy. The kitchen is very hot and having to wear a mask and visor is difficult."

She went on to tell us about a problem that occurred a few days before. "We had several tables booked. A four arrived and were seated by the young waitress. A few minutes later another group of four arrived and greeted the first party. One of the second group began to move a table to join the other party. The boss saw what was happening and immediately stepped in to stop them. He explained that they hadn't booked as a group of eight and therefore couldn't sit together. Fortunately they accepted this and complied when asked to give their contact details in case they needed to be traced in the future."

Another afternoon Penny heard a rumpus coming from the entrance. A party of about seven walkers arrived and asked if they could order afternoon tea. Again, the boss said it would be possible as long as they gave their contact details. The young man who appeared to be in charge refused to give this information, so they were refused admission to the hotel or gardens. Penny felt that her boss was doing things properly. He had consulted the staff during the lockdown and took their views into consideration. He told them that although they wouldn't be making much profit with the current regime- he would be happy if they managed to pay the staff wages and managed to pay for the additional personal protective equipment they had had to buy. Currently he thought it was unlikely that they would make an exception and open during the winter months as the hotel was usually closed then.

The hotel is only booking one bedroom on each floor as there are narrow, rambling corridors snaking along, making social distancing impossible. Cleaning is being done before a new guest arrives but not during their stay. The customer toilets have to be cleaned every hour. The young staff – mainly sixteen and seventeen year olds - were asked to come in with a parent, and the new cleaning regime was explained. If they objected, they would be excused. Whether that meant they wouldn't then have a job wasn't clear, but all the girls accepted the additional duties. Penny thought this was an excellent idea as it meant the staff were on side. Generally business was going steadily and everyone was getting used to their new work regimes.

On a subsequent meeting Mum mentioned she had found it difficult to obtain flour for baking. Penny told us we should have asked her as she could obtain flour in bulk, and she had done shopping for several of the more vulnerable local residents. She said that currently she couldn't get any icing sugar from her wholesale supplier. No doubt, she told us, she could find a suitable substitute. We had no doubt that she would.

A family had been to the hotel that weekend with young children. The parents were allowing their children to wander at random and touch multiple surfaces, including the piano. Penny was called by the young waitress to speak to the parents. Apparently, she asked them to keep their children under control and offered them a cloth and antiseptic to clean the sticky finger marks on the piano. Hopefully the parents will take more responsibility in future.

We didn't see Penny for a long time after this but one day she was all smiles and told us that she was now a grandma. Her son's wife had given birth to a baby girl. She was anxious to tell us that both her son and his wife felt they hadn't been given the usual ante natal training due to the pandemic and they were struggling to get the baby into a routine. Never one to be phased, Penny had Skyped the pair and even demonstrated how to bath the baby. She used one of her daughter's old dolls. It is a pity that Penny and Martin won't get to see their grandchild for some time yet.

Ted and Pauline Taylor

We have always noticed just how active the locals Pauline and Ted are. Until starting this writing course, I had never thought about documenting their existence. They are my Mum and Dad's neighbours in the small village, where they live. The Taylors live in a bungalow opposite them. Come rain or shine you can always guarantee they will be out there. Pauline was once a hairdresser and Ted a builder, a true Yorkshire couple born and bred if ever there was one. Ted is of farming stock in North Yorkshire and Pauline is from a farm around Sutton Bank.

One day, in his typical community spirit, Ted was busy getting rid of weeds on the pavement. This was something that would have never got done had it been left to the local council. Mum and I were out for our daily constitutional walk up the road when we saw Ted. His blue eyes shone brightly beneath his wonderful white, gleaming hair. His infectious smile shone out. 'How are you keeping?', he said. 'I hope that this coronavirus doesn't come here, in other words that nobody from the city comes out to the countryside, or is that narrow minded?', As he completed the arduous task in hand, bent double, he went on to say, 'I do not think Boris is a good leader in these difficult times. Is that ignorant?'

Every Thursday evening many of the villagers would all take part in the NHS clap for carers. Everyone got to know each other much better. It was then that Pauline told us about a pheasant who lives around their dwelling. She had nick-named him, 'Phil'. He had two lady pheasant partners that nest in the bushes of a couple of neighbours. Pauline had seen some eggs in a nest in her large garden. but the hens were not sitting on it. 'It doesn't look like they will have any chicks,' said Pauline. She sounded disappointed. She has also told us numerous stories about other wild creatures who visit her garden, including woodpeckers and tawny owls.

Pauline is slender and well kempt despite undertaking rough jobs requiring appropriate clothing. Both she and Ted like to get stuck in. In the woods beyond the field, Ted and Pauline can often be seen cutting up logs or mending things. This is sometimes in aid of their November 5th fire works party when they build a huge bonfire over the space of two or three months.

There is an abundance of magpies, rabbits and squirrels in the field opposite to my parent's house. We often meet Pauline and Ted in the woods. I think they own some houses which Ted built, as well as the field opposite. The field is often rented out to farmers who put their lambs and sheep to pasture.

Whilst they were building the bungalow opposite, twenty years ago I remember them both climbing frequently on the roof. I was a little unwell at the time, so I remember being a bit spooked. It was out of the ordinary and contrary to what I was used to. Tractor, electric bike, landrover and buggy are the different forms of transport they use. It is a wonder that none of their vehicles have toppled over going down the steep bank which is in their field and popular with local children for sledging during snowy weather.

There is a lady in the village whom we have nicknamed the pheasant. She and her brood of three girls can often be seen walking down the road. She sells jams and cakes from a little stall outside her house by the garden. She reminds us of when we saw a pheasant and chicks outside last year. She was named after a female pheasant was seen followed by her brood of chicks walking down the road and into various local gardens.

Apparently, Pauline and Ted's garden and bungalow are immaculate, though we have never been inside them.

Just before Christmas we noticed activity in the field opposite and just over the wall, so we had a clear view. Ted was fixing something to the ground. Eventually we identified the object as a handmade wooden deer, the next minute a smaller version was placed behind it. Over the next few weeks all who walked past stopped to take selfies with their phones or simply to admire Ted and Pauline's handiwork. A few weeks after Christmas we met Ted with his wheelbarrow as he was about to remove the deer. We persuaded him to leave them a bit longer. One day they disappeared, but Pauline told us to wait to see what would be happening soon.

On the Wednesday of Holy Week we again noticed activity in the same spot and eventually we were introduced to Roger and Ruby Rabbit. The interest they have generated has been fantastic and given so many people something to smile about during these difficult times.

Job Satisfaction

by Karen

He watches the bird as it arrogantly taps its beak against the fence post. He knows he should put on a show of presenting a threat to it- he should leap at it and bring it struggling to the ground in a mess of its own feathers, then drag a selection of its remains into the house. But he lacks the motivation. He is bored with having to display particular behavioural traits in order to maintain a plausible disguise. He senses that the pigeon knows all this as it stares at him, entitled and invincible on the post. Whiskers resents the pigeon. It is not an unfamiliar emotion. He has, of late, felt constantly resentful and bored with everything about his mission. He resents the bland name he has been given by the bland human fools whose lifestyle and habitat he is here on planet Earth to monitor. How unimaginative to name a being after the things protruding from the front of its face. His colleague Minogue, currently residing in a plush apartment in the next street, has been bestowed a far more thrilling moniker by his far more thrilling earthling.

Whiskers resents the bland tinned mush his specimens provide for him to consume, and, on this point, he cannot help but compare himself to Minogue again. Whiskers would never have believed that Minogue indulged in a daily diet of smoked salmon or oven baked tuna steaks, had he not witnessed it for himself on the one occasion when he managed to gain entry to Minogue's flat.

Whiskers feels more resentful than usual today because he has to attend a data sharing meeting, to present this month's findings. These gatherings are a test of his patience because they take place on board the Mothership, which is a pain in the arse to travel to. He would prefer to return to the Planet, where he could at least spend some time with his loved ones after the business of the meeting, but the latest directive from Head office is that the Mothership is an environment more conducive to focusing on the task in hand. 'Head Office' is a phrase borrowed from earthlings, meaning 'Leaders' or 'the Top', presumably because humans have heads at the top of their bodies ponders Whiskers. On our planet, we do not have heads, so this is a peculiar phrase that, in fact, means nothing. As do 'the task in hand' and 'pain in the arse' for that matter. Lost in these thoughts, Whiskers steps right out in front of a car coming towards him at speed.

One down, eight left, he thinks triumphantly before realising- with a degree of resentment- that he is starting to think like a human earthling now.

At the other side of the road, Whiskers meets up with Minogue. He needs only to cast one glance at him to assess that his glamourous associate is in no fit state to attend the meeting, never mind present his findings for the month, which will probably be yet more observation of recreational drug use and the tedious obsession with social media, assumes Whiskers. Minogue is a fool if he thinks he can continue to keep pace with his earthling and all the partying, and there will be trouble again if he can't stay awake during the meeting. As they set off together Minogue is keenly aware of Whiskers' judgemental silence.

On arrival at the Mothership, Whiskers experiences an acute sense of discomfort. The main reason that he hates being here is that, whilst on board, he and his fellow spies are required to remain in feline guise, while their leaders attend in natural form. It is degrading. Whiskers would feel so much more confident and empowered were he able to be himself on these occasions- with his spectacular purple shell and five huge antennae he always commanded the attention of the other genders back on the Planet, but in the role of Whiskers the bland tabby he feels invisible and somehow naked. Minogue, of course, does not suffer such indignity. Resplendent in his new sequinned collar, he is confident and flamboyant as he presents his findings.

As Whiskers had predicted, Minogue's observations of his human this month were all about designer clothing, social media, and party drugs. Such flimsy, superficial nonsense, Whiskers thinks to himself whilst gathering his documents and clearing his throat in preparation for his own moment in the spotlight. He is not looking forward to sharing the latest in his series of papers exploring 'The Dynamics of a Human Family Unit' anticipating that at least one or two of the hundreds of other spies in attendance will want to ask searching questions and get into deep discussion and intellectual analysis. What began as a fascinating research project has lost its appeal for him and he no longer feels driven and passionate about his findings, or those of his colleagues.

"What the hell time do you call this!?" their Commander suddenly shouts, slamming a tentacle down on the desk in front of him. Startled, Whiskers turns to see what has necessitated such an outburst. The Downing Street cat has turned up late, yet again, to his own briefing, an affectation he has recently adopted during the pandemic on earth. Glad of the interruption, Whiskers sits back down in the front row to enjoy the show. The Commander's fourth antennae twitches as he tries to control his temper.

"DO NOT DARE TO PRESUME that being tasked with observing those in government makes you any better than everyone else on this mission!" the Commander shouts. "You would do well to remember that your job is to make observations of humans, not to emulate them! You have never given a straight answer to a simple question ever since you started in your role in Downing Street, and I was prepared to give you the benefit of the doubt, but this keeping everyone waiting for hours on end has gone too far. There are too many of you taking on the characteristics and behaviour of your specimens. And that includes you Minogue. MINOGUE!!! Oh I am sorry, is all this keeping you awake? Yes, YOU!! Do not think that your snazzy collar has escaped my notice. You'll be wearing clothes like him next."

"Like who?" asks Minogue.

"Like your bloody earthling!"

"Well, some earthlings do say that humans and their pets start to look like each other after a while," ventures Minogue, dangerously unaware that this was not a discussion.

"Pets?! Pets??!!" roars the Commander, slamming another tentacle down on his desk. "What the hell is wrong with you?! You are not a pet! Humans might be cretinous enough to believe that you are, but let me remind you of your mission on earth. He turns to the screen behind him, onto which he projects the Team Feline Mission Statement, then reads it aloud: "Team Feline gathers data on the behaviour, values, and beliefs of human earthlings. Our Agents present on earth in feline guise in order to get close to and inside the dwelling places of human beings." Turning back to his audience, he points out that, "Nowhere in the Code of Conduct or your Job Description does it state that 'during their time on earth Agents should behave like or start to resemble their specimens'. Have I made myself clear?"

Whiskers cannot help but bask in a moment of glad satisfaction, pleased that this bone-idle pair of clowns were finally being reprimanded for their self-indulgence. He thinks about Ginger, and how they would have tried to suppress hysterical laughter at the bollocking Minogue and the Downing Street cat were getting. He misses her, and in that moment realises that he has not laughed properly since she left. But his warm glow is short lived, and he soon finds himself on the receiving end of the Commander's wrath too. "And you, Whiskers! Your permanently foul mood and sour attitude have not gone unnoticed. This sneering air of superiority is entirely unprofessional and demotivating for the rest of the team. We will skip your presentation for today, as I'm sure it would only be delivered with a bad grace. See me in my office in half an hour." He scans the crowd. "Tiddles, you can go next, then Carole Baskin. Do either of you have hand-outs to pass round?"

After being sacked from Team Feline, Whiskers successfully applies for a vacant position in the Crop Circles Department, and is happier there than he had ever been in his entire working life. He can really be himself, and sometimes gets the opportunity to flaunt his glistening purple shell and huge naked antennae when he works shirtless in the fields.

He is obviously no longer named Whiskers but goes by the more conventional 'CC202', being the two hundred and second recruit to the Department of Crop Circles. He still resents pigeons - such inconvenient creatures that can cause lengthy delays if they get caught up in the engines when the Craft hovers low above Earth.

Oxtinction: Consequences of the Ungrateful Popullution

by TNX

Being began. Awoken to a crescendo of sensation, transfixed within an ethereal mesmerisation,
In an instance the ecstatic dance of existence entered with little to no resistance.
We were happy. We were strong. Prosperous love, the hollowed-out chorus of our song,
Next, the first to walk and talk stormed then reformed habitations; creatures feared our creation,
Edges pinned each and all within reach, maps were drawn, all was named, et al were claimed.
Then commenced the breathtaking dereliction, whilst failing to savour any delicate temptation,
Appetite was insatiable and as such the feasting continued, unaware what was valuable,
Those *poor* vessels overwhelmed themselves for the bounties before them were incalculable.
...Alas, an era with a paucity of pragmatism gradually ruptured each and every schism,
Ardent believers in the notion of the rapture thought forbidden clung tight to what they were given,
Gaily the rest imbibed the serpent's venom, sniffing short-sighted excitement; mastering inebriation,
Forgiving the sins festering in their corporeal drains, unperturbed by the stains that remained...
The equation was too complex to yet entertain, sole-focus on a momentum they 'had to' maintain,
A mouthful of liquid contained transitioned to an ocean conquered, little fear of rain, nor chilblain,
Fascination to complacency, its use moved to refuse. We learned to disregard our discarded abuse,
Perspective rose; floating up on the dreams of (**their**) dreams, "Welcome!" the future beamed.

If only we had the integrity to believe that this is the air we all breathes final reprieve.
Priorly man learned to smoke, now he forces the affliction upon his helpless under-footing to choke,
Committing an earthly treason, seasons evicted without reason, scorching land we(should)plant trees on,
Ripping out from the root Her leaf support system, suffocating the flora, betraying the fauna,
A cursed eye can spy its own demise in such slaughter. Left to fight only ourselves, as we ought to,
A constellation of contemplation captures the attention, forgotten is the past and all that was asked,
What we learn is overrode by what we yearn, the good outweighed by what we (*might*) earn,
Ladders ascended to bypass any challenge, our foes kicked off –no matter if they land dead,
The jaws of the abyss alerted to their surrender, banking the frail remains of every fallen contender,
Despair to only weep fair in the ebb of tranquillity's disrepair... All is incurably broken.
And thus, a gargantuan body of discontent emerges from the depths, previously unspoken.
Beyond lay a bridge to a bastion on survival's horizon, always assumed to be closer, with_standing,
A crude contamination > being patient, they that swam forever now drown in aphotic tears together.
The shadow of one blocks the Sun like a mountain, his ballistic fallacies spraying like a fountain,
Facts have served their purpose only to breed jealousy, a new 'real' uncovered; modernised heresy,
Now, we're just waiting... and, weighting ...too long to intervene ...too late to save our Omniqueen.

Forced into a false demise, the 'limit' of self willingly realised, "the future belongs to a new guise!",
The olive branch downed so the blade could rise. Heaven's destruction meticulously authorised,
The sky will turn black before dusk, for evermore, an **unliveable** atmosphere of rust, forever more,
All feelings die in that perma-fog, a heart already usurped by a battery, no longer desires of flattery,
Inhale/exhale no more essential, only the lifeless will live to respire from their iron lungs of irony,
Earth's (e)motions will run dry, victims to be vilified for the courage in hearing Her swan-song cry,
As entirety takes Her final breath, folly bestowed unto the hierarchy left; the forsaken unawakened.
The precious gift we took, would be a mistake mistook, and all just for those three tragic words:
Earth... Can't... ... Breathe...
The spectacle projected onto her suffering celestial siblings, known only as *Her* Seven Witnesses.
In the wake of a dream gone awry, the last death underlines the ultimate existential damnation.
Will we seem just a singular Event? A burning invitation sent, leaving ourselves no time to repent,
Entropy at its finest, and ending our descent. As Earth as it is to lay in dust our betrayal in Her
Trust...
Ends with merely a patter... If only we could have shown that **we** can be just as tolerant as **she**,
Earth... Can't... ... Breathe... Earth... Can't... ... Breathe... Earth... Can't... ... Breathe...

This is Our Space
by Lucy Waters

No one can deny 2020 was a year like no other. A turbulent rollercoaster ride, stuck on repeat, the operator absent for an extended break. To put it quite simply, Christmas 2019 - we had no idea. Love, laughter, family time. Cocooned in the warm familiarity of Christmases past, senses flooded with the sounds and smells uniquely synonymous with the time of year. In our joy and revelry, we were oblivious to an invisible enemy halfway around the world. A war brewing, the likes of no other seen before. Nature's biological battle far beyond our control, a battle that would change lives, change the world forever.

Spring

Never have I experienced fear on a scale such as this. Consuming my every waking moment, I am trapped by the binding tendrils of anxiety. My stomach a twisted knot. Body struck rigid with every news report. A mountain evolved from a rock on the horizon now clouds my vision. We dance to a different beat. Shielding, furlough, social distance, a new vocabulary now rolls from the tongue with the familiarity of language inherited from birth, but it's not. Stay at home, save lives is the mantra we now live by. But I have to break free.

"It's just nice to be out, isn't it?" I look up as a voice to my right disturbs my reverie. There's a man a similar age to me with a small dog and a bright yellow tennis ball with one of those long sticks I've seen used to fling the ball as far as possible.

"It is," I reply with a hesitant smile. "I needed a change of scenery."

"I'm just thankful he gets me out." The man nods towards his dog. He launches the tennis ball far out across the green and the little dog hurtles after it. We smile at each other, nod and move away, continuing on our own solitary escape missions. I walk along the edge of the green feeling the soft grass beneath my feet and breathe the earthy smell whipped up by recent rain and the cooling air as evening rushes in. As I walk, I watch the little dog playing with his ball, skidding, running and catching. I smile wistfully to myself; thinking of my mum's little dog and wondering when we will play ball again. I feel a tug in my chest and I push the thought away and avert my gaze before my eyes begin to prickle. It doesn't take much these days for the tears to brim and fall.

Feeling reckless yet cautiously determined I perch on the edge of the bench. My tense body unwilling to relinquish fully, lest too much relaxation perforates my bubble, my shield. I'm puzzled. Ten years of living just three minutes' walk away; why I haven't previously given this space the validity it so effortlessly deserves. A simple triangular expanse of grass spreads out before me, edged with a simple wooden fence, flat in the middle but rising with different gradients on two sides. A children's play area furnishes the eastern edge whilst the south side climbs steeply with deep stone steps carved into the slope. It's a curious location and surveying the nearby buildings I cannot help but wonder of the stories they could tell.

Another day, another bench and here I am again. My space. My happy place. What started out as a one-time rebellion from my shielding fortress has now become ritual. A sense of peaceful release descends upon me as I sit, paused in a moment's distraction from a world now upside down. With repeated guilt I still cannot comprehend my previous lack of appreciation for this little oasis. A space largely unremarkable on the surface, but delve a little deeper and there are plenty of hidden treasures. There's the war memorial at the top of the green, powerfully poignant, standing to attention and keeping watch. A now defunct drinking fountain idles sadly as a rusty plaque announces a royal legacy and provokes intrigue into the life this space once knew. I smile to myself at the irony of this discovery. I'm not quite sure how a public shared drinking fountain would fare today in Covid Britain!

Time has slowed and life has been stripped back. We are watching and waiting, ears listening, eyes open and arms stretched wide. But nature isn't waiting, and it certainly won't hide. A solitary black planter stands in equal isolation, hovering awkwardly, an outsider wanting to fit in.

In garish boldness primroses make their voice known. Pink and purple, orange and white, their delicate silky petals nestle amongst waxy wrinkled leaves. A flower, a leaf, an insect or a tree; the slowing of time and life's busy embrace has fostered a new appreciation of the little things. Back to basic and pure simplicity, I notice 'more' and relish the tiny details. The silver lining to my heavy cloud.

I continue my wanderings day by day. Finding a rhythm, needing the familiarity and routine when life is anything but. Morning, afternoon and evening I visit at all times of the day, breathing deep, soaking up the air and loosing myself in bird song and the distant hum of traffic, before I return to my enforced captivity. The more I come the more I realise I'm not the only one who needs this space. There's the lady with the purple anorak and the little white dog. They come here daily, I think. Home workers out for a lunchtime stroll, seeking a new normal whatever that may be. Then there's dad and son, always serious, engaged in self-imposed football training, no doubt a substitution for matches now postponed. Cross words exchange and there's a stomp of feet. You can feel their emotion, their frustration. Our frustration.

Summer

Golden rays cascading far and wide. Day after day and week after week the sun has shone. A now predictable relief, the weather is our only certainty amongst so many unknowns. Once a vivid green, the grass is now parched like straw matting, dry to the bone.

But things are changing beyond my control and it's hard not to feel protective of this sanctuary of mine. Irritation gnaws at me tensely as I carve out my steady route, determinedly dodging and picking my way amongst intruders too wrapped up in their social revelry and oblivious to my toe-curling anxiety.

Daytimes are tricky and I still need some relief. Visiting in the evening I find much needed peace, wandering beneath the trees with the grass tickling my toes as the sun makes a blushing retreat. Swallows swoop and call, arching a perfect silhouette in the warm viscous sky. I am alone and at peace as I watch nature bringing an end to its day. I draw a line and replace the lid bringing closure to mine too, before turning, homeward bound, to the walls of my nest, safe and secure. I'm one step closer and tomorrow is near.

Autumn

Today is a triumph not to be ignored. I'm back, I'm here, in my 'oh so happy' place once more! With quiet relief the school term is underway and finally daily life has a slight resonance of routine. Lost to my thoughts I shuffle along with hope and optimism. It's much quieter, calm and still. I would be lying if I said I wasn't relieved by the renewed silence. Just lately I've seen a shift, subtle at first but growing steadily like a ship on the horizon. A person too close, a group too large, a touch or a hug that just shouldn't be. A blind eye turned but not by me.

Gone are the picnics and sticky ice lollies. Absent are the children, their groups and their games. Missing are the playground giggles and shrieks, as though time and nature have pressed pause. The solitary swings gently jiggle and sway, while from the slide the sun's reflection delivers a daring, tempting wink. Maybe one day. I smile.

This morning there's a cool nip in the air but a warmth of colour nibbles the edges of the trees. Our first glimpse of nature's preparation for what is yet to come. It's an early start but with childlike pleasure I feel the first leaves crinkle and crunch beneath my feet. My favourite season. My favourite place.

Steely grey clouds hang heavily ominous overhead. It's cold, its dark, its damp and just downright miserable. I stride with purpose; I'll not be beaten. I'm keeping my routine and I'm keeping my freedom. It's all falling apart but I'm clutching a rope. Fluffy socks and cosy toes, scarf wrapped tight and hood pulled close in a soft cocoon. Through my boots I feel the ground resist, a solid permanence I need when my world feels so off kilter.

The leaves clump together and they stick to my feet while the naked branches shiver overhead. Matching the nation's mood, a relentless rain leaks from the sky and I have to tip toe to avoid the worst of squelches. Slowing my pace to avoid a soggy disaster I lift my head to peek out beneath my hood. I'm alone, almost. I'm the only one here today except for a solitary dog walker treading with persistence along the perimeter, lead in hand, tugging with urgency each time his four-legged friend stops for a sniff. Amongst the raindrops no one notices the hot, angry tears stinging my cheeks. Silent and invisible they merge and dilute. I sit and I stare and I drink it all in. In soggy companionship I need this space and I think it needs me.

Winter

Winter arrives and nature's fragility is naked and exposed. Life is taking a different spin once more, the world upside down, and earth's axis on a different spin. It's New Year's Eve and I stand at the top of the slope looking down over the green, on a precipice, waiting and hoping but resigned to what is yet to come. The trees shiver without their leafy cloak and bare branches stand out against an icy pink sunset. The slushy remains of yesterday's snow are now frozen into crunchy crystals but this hasn't deterred the families determinedly sledging down the steep bank. Sheltered from the sun for much of the day this side of the green holds its own little microclimate, colder and icier than the rest of the space. Shrieks of laughter, shouting and joy. Parents stand to watch, capturing photos, smiling and laughing, making memories and joining in.

The earth feels hard as stone today as I tiredly trek on autopilot towards my chosen bench. In that post Christmas slump, I have escaped my fortress once more, on a mission to lift myself up, renew my strength and close a door on 2020 one last time. To my right I smile as two friends meet on a bench. Far apart yet gloriously together they hug the air and settle down with picnic glasses in gloved hands to toast the New Year, determined to share this moment no matter the weather or the restrictions.

I watch the sledging for a while and spot a few familiar faces amongst the brave dog walkers picking their way through the frozen grass. Some smile and say hello when they pass, whether in recognition or courtesy I don't really mind. The human contact is enough. As darkness descends I begin my walk home. Slipping and sliding on the glassy pavements I beat a hasty retreat, ready to batten down the hatches and face the storm that is ahead.

It's bitingly cold and icy but I don't care. All day I've watched and I've waited until the snow began to fall and when it did I waited and watched some more. Gradually the stunted stems of grass outside my window were cloaked in a white blanket and I know it's time. Cautious but determined I set out for my special place, wanting to capture this memory and appreciate winter's beautiful show. As I approach I see a couple of families with their wellies on, hats pulled down over their ears, heading in only one direction. Our space. Growing louder, in the distance I can hear the shouts and shrieks once more.

I enter beneath the trees where the snowy carpet is patchier. A childlike glow forms deep inside me as I step out into the open and feel the snowy powder creak beneath my feet. Watching my feet leaving perfect imprints in the clean snow I carve a different route today. There will be no skirting the perimeter beneath sheltered trees, no benches to sit on or steps to climb. I want to be in the open, to feel the snowflakes flutter against my face. I'm here to drink it all in and store it away, a beauty to behold, far removed from tragedy and fear as biological war rears its ugly head once more. Recently I've appreciated peace in abundance here in my winter solace and have waited and hoped for this day to make my heart complete. I survey the scene as more and more families arrive and quietly observe a transformation as they and I are lifted from winter's grey and tired monotony. My glass is no longer half empty and my cup is full, I am sustained and ready to ride the rollercoaster once more.

Spring again

Sitting in my favourite spot, legs swinging pendulum like, betraying a nervous joy. There's a feeling of freedom, a weight from my shoulders, as I breathe in the cool spring air and survey the familiar yet strikingly different scene. There is an air of hope and renewal as though I am standing on a precipice ready to take a leap. Sunlight shrouds me in gentle warmth, gold rays lapping the edges of my solid sculpted fear. The dark clouds scudding across the surface of my mind are clearing, opening up to the piercing blue expanse of sky.

It's hard not to feel protective and as I survey the greatly increasing number of people I feel my toes clench a little once more. I anxiously fiddle and flip my new lanyard; bright green with sunflowers, there is a message needing to be told. Please give me space, just let me be. My little place of quiet and solitude is evolving once more.

Squeeze through the gap in the hedge and dodge the puddle if you can. A canopy of leaves, recently unfurled, awakening the trees from their sleepy winter slumber, now adorns the northern entry. I feel their shelter and protection and I'm enveloped by familiarity and contented joy. My pace quickens downhill as I scuff my trainers through newly laid bark, earthy and spongy beneath my feet. The wind rushes and whispers high above as I make my descent. It's been a little while since my last visit and I see it's not just my life, which has sprung forth. Beneath the trees in a sheltered corner the bluebells softly tickle and sway while the drooping daffodils have begun their slow retreat.

Thump! Suddenly I'm falling, tumbling, swirling backwards, a whirlpool in my mind. A frothy wave of emotions washes over me as I fight the flickering pictures inside my head. That one little blue flower is all it takes. I'm there, right back where it all began, one year ago. The tight knot in my stomach, body frozen ridged and toes curled in my shoes. A voice in my head: "Breathe. Breathe. You can do this!"

Searching for comfort, my eyes scan from left to right and back again. With glorious relief my gaze locks upon my goal. I'm here, I'm here and so are they, some are missing and some are not. Life is moving on, stepping forward and breaking free. I know their names now. Tracey ambles along, little Alfie trundling and sniffing not far behind. Tracey has a new coat and Alfie a new lead, a fresh start and a new beginning.

All around me life seems to be gathering pace, spreading out and broadening its wings, unfolding like a butterfly emerging from a chrysalis. The playground buzzes as children dart from place to place, an exercise class and a game of football in open space. So many firsts, so fresh and new. The cafe is doing a roaring trade of picnic boxes, cakes, sandwiches and hot drinks and people are competing for benches or sprawl relaxed on brightly coloured blankets. All this freedom and sense of belonging, rejoining, connecting as we learn to 'do life' once more. And although my horizons are broadening and the boundaries removed, I know that right here on my doorstep this is my space. This is our space.

I'd Like to Play Guitar and other poems

by Mary C Palmer

I'd like to play guitar

I'd like to play the guitar
And sing along to the sound
Adding music to my words
To find a new love found

To hear the notes
Learn how to play
To soothe my soul
And have control
As my music plays
Feeling the harmonies sway

To hear the sound of my music
And loving every chord
Soothing my soul
Adding my own word

To share with you
As I play along
The new music
And words
To my song

To play for you
So you could hear
And feel the loving too.

Me

I wanna dance
I wanna sing
I wanna love
Everything

I wanna feel love
I wanna feel
Someone
Love me

I wanna love Someone
Someone who loves me
I wanna dance
I wanna sing
I wanna open my wings
I wanna fly on the wind

I wanna swing
I wanna sing
I wanna dance
I want Love & romance
I wanna learn a new dance
I wanna take a chance
On love & romance

Someone to love me

Wild and free
To feel
To touch
To hear
Someone say
This way
I love you so much

I wanna shake up my life
And give me a chance
I wanna push my pace
I wanna run the race
I wanna run through the rain
I wanna fight all the pain
I wanna fight the wrong
I wanna be sturdy n strong
I wanna fight for tomorrow
I wanna lose all the sorrow

I want to find me
Just you wait n see
Me

No more acting like the fools
No more breaking all the rules
I'll sleep by night
And eat good by day
Water will cleanse
My inner me
In every way

And I will work hard

To chase, to erase
The old day away
You'll see
One day.

Joey

Oh how I still
Remember you
The beautiful you
That I once knew

I remember how
You held me
And the excitement
In each kiss
The teenage passion
We shared
Was pure bliss

I thought it was forever
And how
It would always
Be like this

How time has flown by
So, so far
And I still wonder
How you are

Still wonder
what might have been

In the story
Of you and me

And I wonder
If, you remember me
The girl, I used to be
Me.

The Last Great Bin Find

by Kevin Keld

I have always had a fascination with articles from a previous era, or junk as some might call it. Forget the modern fad for 'upcycling' or recycling, I have been doing all that since the early 1970s. As a child of ten-years-old I would mount my trusty racing bicycle, resplendent with its red taped handlebars and bright red metalflake saddlebag then head off in the direction of the Yorkshire Wolds in search of artefacts from a bygone era. I had earmarked three places on the Wolds that frequently offered up quirky and interesting discoveries amongst the discarded Ford Escort vans and empty drums of foul-smelling chemicals. In retrospect it's scary to think of the dangerous situations I would put myself in. Clambering down mountains of jagged steel and glass to seek out and rescue an old radio or gramophone then have to balance it precariously on my shoulders and negotiate the sheer cliffs of rubbish with the dogged determination of a mountain climber. I would then attempt to affix the aforesaid items to the top of the flimsy saddlebag then attempt the arduous journey back home via a hill on par with Ben Nevis. I could easily touch 40mph down this hill (I know that because for my tenth birthday my uncle bought me a speedometer for my bike, and from that day onwards I would attempt to cycle down every hill in the area to try and beat the top speed setting of 60mph).

After a while, I had amassed a dilapidated garden shed full of junk, TVs that didn't work, broken tools and an assortment of electronic devices some of which I had no idea what their purpose was. They may have had the outward appearance of a 1950s valve radio but my imagination transformed them into critical parts of the Starship Enterprise. My first love though was for musically related gadgets. Old radios with valves, tape recorders, amplifiers to name but a few. I would study books and magazines to try and learn the basics of electronics repair but mostly relied on just cutting random wires and sticking rusty screwdrivers into the back of a radio and hoping for the best. This often ended in a flash, a bang and my mother running up the yard shouting that the electricity had gone off...again.

I had once retrieved sufficient electronic devices to attempt to create my own Doctor Who's Tardis. I eagerly explained to all my friends what I was planning to build and they would be more than welcome to join me on a jaunt back to the 1850s or into the far future of the 2000s to search for the Daleks. I was deadly serious but judging by some of the looks they all thought I had been eating far too many sherbet pips and penny chews for my own good. I never did finish the Tardis and it too succumbed to the flash, bang and the voice of Mother dearest bellowing, "Kevin, what ARE you doing down there?"

My affection for recycling old items continued well into my adult life and I was the proud owner of Kevin Keld Motorcycles, a two-wheel emporium of spare parts and old motorcycles that had gained 'end of life' status. I would either restore the machines to their former glory or break them down into parts to re-sell for spares. I made a hell of a lot of money from my hobby/business and the profits even stretched to buying me a fine property in Southern Spain where I spent a fantastic ten years...recycling. In fact, I grabbed the recycling bug by the horns and immersed myself in yet more abandoned projects. I initially used the popular 'rastro's' or markets to sell off the excess stock I had left over from furnishing the house. This was easy money and I could get used to this. No worries about being stood behind a market stall on a dark cold wet day in February like back in Blighty. It was mostly blue skies and sunny days when I had to lounge in a deck chair watching the endless stream of customers passing through, all willing to hand over hard-earned holiday cash for some of the tat I had accumulated. Unfortunately for me, the tat was running out pretty quickly so I devised a route around the local urbanizations diligently searching their waste skips for cast-off furniture and goodies. I would find with incredible regularity whole kitchen suites, antique furniture, sofas, TVs and on one visit a large box of sealed blocks of cheese direct from the local Aldi. Even if the items were broken they would be all hauled into the van to be taken back to my workshop for repair and restoration, then they would be put on display at the next market with a decent price tag.

One particular Saturday morning I was fully loaded in the van with not a single centimetre of space available and spied an antique wooden table with six upholstered chairs on route to the market. Not one to be outdone I managed to procure enough rope and ratchet straps to secure it albeit loosely to the roof of the van. I didn't even have to unload it, the minute I arrived at my pitch two old Moroccan guys insisted on buying the lot for 100 euros and even unloaded it for me, no mean feat in the baking, sweaty thirty-degree sunshine. On another trip to the skips in the wonderful town of Marbella, I procured a large painting. It was an extremely large painting too, measuring ten feet high and four feet wide. The subject matter was rather striking too, a semi-naked lady with eyes like pools of green silk on a beautiful blue background, I felt sure I had attended school with her some forty years ago but perhaps that was my vivid imagination working overtime again. The painting, quite understandably attracted lots of admirers when it was displayed on my market stall the following week but I was just looking for that one ardent admirer with plenty of money in their pockets. I didn't have to wait long before an impeccably dressed chap from a local antique shop handed over three hundred Euros for the pleasure of owning the beautiful painting.

I could go on forever with the deals and finds that I managed to get myself involved with over the ten-year stint in Spain but the main subject of this little story is the very last bin find. You must forgive my wanderings as I get far too excited and carried away with the success of the 'skip diving'. It was the very last day I was to be on Spanish soil, my wife had left the country four weeks previously to seek out suitable employment and a place to live back in the homeland.

This left my son William and me to load up the van and trailer with the remainder of our belongings. Most of the larger furniture had been sold on the sales running up to the final day in the quaint little church house we had lived in for the past three years, which left us with the smaller items, the clothes and my two motorcycles in the trailer. Whilst we are on the subject of clothes I simply must relate this tale too. My wife had previous to her departure sorted her best clothes from the ragged and oversized items and had packed her finest dresses and shoes in a suitcase and leaving a black bin bag full of items that no longer fitted her or were out of fashion. In my eagerness to get the van loaded I threw in the black bag and later in the day when I asked my son to see what was in the suitcase left in the garage he assured me that it was full of old clothes. So, and I simply know you are miles ahead of me now, I landed in England with a black bin liner full of old, unfashionable clothes whilst the best evening dresses and designer tops sat in a suitcase on a massive heap of rubbish left in our yard. It cost me in the long run though because I had to buy her a new wardrobe full of glittery frocks and dresses!

Anyhow back to the story in hand, we were to leave our property and head up to Bilbao to catch the ferry back to Portsmouth. I had allowed a week to travel back allowing my son and me a chance to chill out on the journey, with overnight stays to take in the sights of Madrid and Burgos. Ooo...I have another story about almost losing the trailer in a hotel car park in Madrid but I'll save that for another day but in case I forget just give me a nudge. It's at this point in my story that things get a little more interesting. Early morning on the day of the great exodus I popped up to the local fuel station on the outskirts of Alhaurin to say my goodbyes and fill up the vehicle with diesel. As I turned right off the main road from Fuengirola to Alhaurin on the way back to the church, I noticed that someone had dumped an old sofa, some kitchen units and an old suitcase at the skip at the end of our lane. Of course, I had to stop and have an inspection of the goodies but concluded that I really didn't have space for this rubbish in the van or trailer so with great reluctance I had to drive away and leave it. I collected my son and we headed off in the direction of England and once again as I passed the bins I was drawn to tempting looking cast-offs. Everything appeared to have been part of a very old house clearance but yet again I failed to convince myself to shoehorn the bits into the trailer. Being the good Samaritan that I am I made a phone call to a friend who was also on the same market circuit and we often shared a pitch at the La Cala Rastro held at the racecourse every Sunday. I told him of the find at my own skip and as he only lived a few kilometres away he would come straight out with the van to take a look.

I was actually in France when I received the dreaded call. How come you were in France? I hear you all say. Well, after we eventually made our way to the ferry terminal in Bilbao via two very interesting overnight stays in Burgos and Madrid, I was pulled aside by the Guardia Civil. This would not normally cause distress as I am not one for hiding copious amounts of class A drugs in my van or indeed gun running but on this particular van search the officer was disturbed by the dog I was carrying. Not a Rottweiler or nasty pit bull I might add but a meek and well-mannered sausage dog. My wife's dog, a Dachshund aptly named Romeo. The officer, in his best Sunday voice, snapped, "Papers," and it was at this point I realised that the papers we had were out of date by a month. I could have perhaps coped with the rejection had he been a tad more friendly and instead of barking, "Papers," could have merely said, "Now lad, 'ow yer doin? I don't suppose I could take a peek at your paperwork, could I?" There was no way on earth was that officer going to allow us to board the ferry, the ferry that was leaving in two hours! Frantically the officer advised that if the dog were to have suitable injections then we would be let on board. I began the search for a vet in the town of Bilbao on a Sunday afternoon. It was to prove hopeless and I am sure it would have been easier to find someone full of red wine and doing impersonations of a sausage dog than a vet that would answer the phone. I was faced with the option of missing the voyage or changing the ticket for another day. I plumped for the latter. Unfortunately, it wouldn't set sail for another seven days. Damn, damn and double damn. The good news was that our tickets could be changed to depart from Le Havre in France and they wouldn't be so adamant about having the correct papers. We pointed the van, the trailer and the dog in the general direction of Le Havre and hit the road as soon as humanely possible. Hence why I was in France, well Le Mans to be precise when my buddy Paul rang with the punchline to this long eventful story. Personally, I would have been grateful if he hadn't called at all. I knew I was heading for disappointment when the first words he uttered were, "Kev, you know that load of old junk you were too idle to collect by the skips?" I didn't even answer but awaited his descriptive, gloat-filled story.

Yes, he had taken my advice and taken his van to the skip and yes, the vintage furniture and assorted knick-knacks were still there. He chose to abandon the old furniture in favour of a few of the smaller items and the age-old suitcase. Whoever had owned the case had certainly been well travelled, it was adorned with stickers and badges dating back decades from the places the owner had visited: Paris, Bangkok, Dewsbury to name but a few. I lied about the last destination though. When Paul arrived at his house he had just dropped off the junk and made a mental note to sort through it later that week. He almost threw the case back in the skip but something made him investigate further. It was filled with old clothes and these were thrown in the washer to repurpose and taken to one of the many charities operating in Southern Spain. After emptying the case he heard something rattle in it. Initially, nothing was visible but after shaking the case he heard the distinct noise of something moving around in the lining. This was a very old case and built well and had the lining fully stitched all around. Taking a knife he cut a slit of around six inches in the lining and shook the case again. Out dropped a bag full of assorted rings and bracelets. He immediately thought that he had found a bag of dress jewellery but imagine his surprise when upon closer inspection they were gold, platinum and diamonds. He couldn't believe his good fortune but the search wasn't over yet. That poor suitcase was destroyed in his vigorous search for more golden eggs. He didn't have to wait long before tearing open the bottom lining and there, rolled up in a plastic bag was a wad of Euros, in fact, there were four thousand Euros. Included in the haul was four gold necklaces too.

When he told me I felt sick and dizzy and had to compose myself. He had the rings appraised and the whole find came to just over nine thousand Euros. Let me say that once more, very slowly, N-I-N-E T-H-O-U-S-A-N-D Euros. I still to this day cannot believe that it was the only time I never took advantage of something abandoned near the skip. The rest of the journey back to the UK was somewhat of a sombre affair though filled with enough adventures to fill a book. You really must ask me about them sometime.

Maeve Quinn

By Esther Clare Griffiths

Chapter 1
The Long Night

I remember how it began. One night everything changed. Somehow, I managed to drive home through the dark winding lanes with their tall primrose banks. Already flashbacks of the car park cast shadows across my mind. I kept glancing in my mirror to see if he was following me – if he drove without lights, I wouldn't see him in the pitch black. My eyes strained to see the road edges, there were no cat's eyes, no streetlights, just never-ending night. Perhaps this was a version of hell. Perhaps I was trapped in my dad's car, doomed to drive through the twists and turns of the road ahead, forever steeped in darkness. *You've a flair for the drama, Maeve, so you have. Sure, we're two peas in a pod* – Eliza's voice whispered in my ear, on and on, like the sea at night. But I was all alone in the heart of County Antrim, in the middle of nowhere. Scarcely a soul lived beyond the tight hedges and black banks. I sped up, taking the corners with reckless haste. I had to get home, fast. My hands felt tight on the wheel. I had a vision of my beautiful daughter, Marlena rolling her eyes, *'Oh Mum! Really?'* I almost smiled and for a second, my hands uncurled and slid a little down the steering wheel. I could see my cold clammy finger marks on the plastic, and I felt sick from all the tight bends, sick from fear. My hands tightened their grip again, my knuckles white in the darkness. Sinister clouds seemed to beckon me from above cold hilltops, but I looked away. I forced my eyes back to the road ahead. *What if I crashed into the steep banks and never reached home? Or worse still, what if Marlena discovered what I had done?*

Even in the town, it was too late for streetlights. But I knew the houses, I knew every swerve in the road by heart. I still had a sense he was following me, and my eyes stayed glued to the mirror, searching for a car behind. At last, I pulled up by our house and turned off the engine. Quiet spread out around me, infusing the whole night – even my breathing matched the silence. Shallow, anxious breaths, without depth. I couldn't really breathe, and I felt utterly alone - like I was the only person awake, the only person tormented with a secret. Not a single light left on in any of the squashed-up terraces tumbling out across our valley. *Was the whole town fast asleep?* Maybe all of Ireland was sleeping still, slumbering unawares. I opened the car door and closed it quietly. My eyes darted across the street, I mustn't wake the neighbours. They would wonder why on earth I was home in the dead of night. Tiptoeing up the path, my feet gathered speed and I tore up the steps to my home. I fumbled for the key, my heart racing fast, like a song played at the wrong speed. My daughter's shoes and coat were by the door, she was home safe. I let myself breathe out. Sure, Marlena would set me straight in the morning. I glanced out the window, but I could see nothing in the black night. Just darkness stretching on over invisible rooftops and silent sleeping hillsides.

I stumbled onto my bed, burrowing down under my covers to escape the icy air, to escape the truth. I gradually felt the cold slipping away, the warmth of my body finally de-icing the bed. I waited for sleep to lift me away. But my mind just wouldn't let me go. I kept thinking of how on earth I was going to explain my way out of the whole mess. *How on earth could I get away with it? Was he alright? He was bound to be angry. Surely, someone would find out, someone would find out it was me. It was really just a matter of time.* I tossed and turned, my stomach in knots until I knew I wasn't going to fall asleep. Swinging my legs out of bed, I reached for my dressing gown and snuck down our creaky stairs. The last thing I wanted was to wake my baby girl, Marlena. Of course, eleven could hardly be seen as a baby, but still, she was just a waif, so young, so quick to take on the world. For a moment, I let it cross my mind what she would feel if she knew. My heart sped up. I couldn't let myself go down that road. *No, I must make sure she never, ever found out. She would see me so differently, maybe she wouldn't love me anymore.* I shuddered and took my tea back upstairs, missing the creaky steps. With a cup of tea circling my hands, I felt better. Perhaps it wasn't so bad. Perhaps I could find some way out. One in which I could still look at myself in the mirror.

While I was watching the steam from my cuppa curling into icy air, I heard a knock. So faint I thought it was a creature outside. But then I heard it again. Three gentle taps at our back door. *Oh God, was it him? Was he here to have it out with me once and for all?* I peered out the window, my eyes straining to make out anything in the dark. Frost was already sparkling its cold breath over every paving stone and every blade of grass. Then I saw her. I knew who it was instantly. The stoop of her shoulders, the bony frame and long grey hair. My adoptive mother – my real mother, Theresa. Any inkling of sleepiness vanished. I ran quickly down the stairs, holding my breath, as if that would make the blindest bit of difference. With a bit of luck, Marlena would stay fast asleep. Scrabbling for the key, I tried to stay calm, I tried to stop my heart speeding out of control. *Surely Theresa wasn't here to talk about last night? How on earth could she possibly know?* My hands were back to ice and my fingers were stiff, like the blood had frozen solid. *What on earth was Theresa doing here?* It must be urgent for her to be knocking on our door in the wee small hours. I peeled back the door and felt the rush of icy air hit my face. I stepped back instinctively.

'Come away on in Mother. Sure, you must be freezing. I'll put the kettle on.'

Eliza always said Nana made a pot of tea before talking of anything important – as though all ills could be faced with a cuppa in hand. Here I was following in her footsteps. Theresa was sitting at my kitchen table, just as I had sat at hers for almost twenty years. Her lips were white with a touch of blue around the edges. God, she was chilled to the bone. I placed a blanket over her shoulders and gave her a tight hug. She smelled of the cold night air and her kitchen – a mixture of bleach, baking and castor oil. She smelled of home and for a few seconds I forgot all about the night before. I chose my best cups, white with tiny yellow flowers, and covered the teapot in the crocheted tea cosy Theresa made long ago. It was no longer cream, more of a dusty beige, fraying slightly at the edges. I focussed on not letting my hand shake as I poured the tea, and we listened in silence as it slurped gently into the cups. Dark, ochre liquid, deep as the great slabs from our peat bogs. Theresa looked suddenly tiny in the dim light, her outline traced in shadows across the wall. I reached for her hands across the table and tried to gently squeeze them warm. They were ice cold and wrinkled - rough skin so familiar, my eyes prickled with tears. *Was she very lonely?* I must visit her more often. The weeks fled so fast, I could scarcely keep up. Guilt clawed its way into me, and I stared at her hands, gritting my teeth to stop the tears. I waited. *What was she going to say?* Anxiety dripped slow and then fast, fast, fast like a runaway train picking up speed. My hands pressed hard into the sides of my teacup. I scarcely felt the heat. Theresa held hers gingerly by the handle. I bit my lip. The kitchen clock seemed to beat louder and louder. I had to crane my head to hear Theresa's words.

'It's your… your ma… it's Eliza. She's taken ill and is asking to see you. I promised I would come and let you know right away. But the bus was so late, I had to come at this God-forsaken hour. I'm sorry, Margaret.'

Even now, she calls me Margaret, even when I had chosen Maeve – Eliza's name for me. It had felt right at the time. Now I wasn't so sure. For a moment I was flooded with relief – *Theresa didn't know about last night*. But then my heart sank. I was still more than a little afraid of Ma's illness – it transformed her into someone else, someone I didn't even recognise. As a child, I'd been terrified. I would watch her become wide-eyed, her hair wild and her speech slurred, like she had been taken over by the devil. I was so scared she wouldn't come back to me, so afraid I would lose her forever. And that was before I knew who she really was.

Chapter 2
My Mother

Of course, for most of my childhood, I didn't know Eliza Quinn was my real birth mother. I thought she was just a friend of Theresa's. Sure, sometimes I felt it was strange they lived together, two women bringing up children – it wasn't exactly the norm in Northern Ireland in the 1920s and 30s. It still rankled with me that Theresa knew nothing. Out of the goodness of her heart, she had taken Eliza in, let her live with us. Even when she was bullied by others at church, she still stood by my birth mother. Maybe Eliza was like a daughter to her. Maybe she didn't want to see the truth.

'I know it's hard on you, Margaret love, but she would love to see you. You mean the world to her. Sinead is up from Dublin, so you would have a chance to see her too.'

Sinead, Eliza's best friend, an aunty to me, a rock to us all. When I moved away from home, she often came to see me. Always with a good word about Eliza. I loved Sinead. I loved Eliza too, I just couldn't stand to be with her. She had let me down, I couldn't really trust her. *Sure, who spins out a lie for so many years? Who lives with people and lies to their faces every single day?* I shift uncomfortable, seeing a parallel with my own life. I too am hiding the truth from my daughter. The panic starts to rise up again, I squash it away. Theresa is watching me. I know those worry lines across her forehead, I know those grey eyes, always so sad. I look away.

'Sure, I'll go and see her at the weekend, I can't skip work.'

Another lie. I can easily take time off work – after all, I'm the library manager. I can't meet Theresa's eye, I get up to boil the kettle again, this time for hot water bottles. Without looking at Theresa, I begin hauling blankets out of the cupboard, pillows from my bed and a clean sheet. I make up the sofa. Our eyes meet for a moment when I hand her the hot water bottle. She smiles and I force the corners of my mouth to curl at the edges. Theresa holds the bottle to her chest, like a protective barrier.

'You know, I have come to terms with what Eliza did. It's time for you to listen to the good Lord and forgive her. Sure, you'll feel better, so you will.'

The good Lord? I bite my lip. *Where was the good Lord when I needed him? Nowhere!* I nod briefly and wish her goodnight. Then I turn away and creep back upstairs to my cold bed. My cold sheets seem to whisper, *forgive her, forgive her*. I cover my ears and burrow down in the bed, as though I might find a secret escape tunnel. A passage to safety, away from the sinking chasm of my pain.

When I was a little girl, Eliza would take me to a stream where we dipped our toes and watched the fishes. Sometimes in my dreams, I go back there. Only instead of dipping my toes, they begin to be sucked beneath the current. I always wake before I go under completely. I know it means something, I know it speaks volumes, but I don't want to know in case the flood gates open. I swallow hard. There is no way I am ever going to let myself go under like my mother. I have seen her disappear for months at a time, dragged down so deep, no one can pull her out. I remember the first time she was really ill, I painted her a picture. I was so excited to see her face light up and even waited for the right moment to hand it over. My pride had me almost bursting at the seams. I thought Eliza was easily the best artist in the whole of Ireland, sure, she was the best in the whole wide world. The painting I loved most was of glossy green fields, stretching up from a valley, with black trees silhouetted over each horizon, like a warning. When no one was looking, I would trace my fingers through the scores of gloopy, thick paint. I tried to copy it, sweeping the brush across the paper in big, bold swathes – just like I'd watched Eliza paint countless times before. I added me and Eliza, holding hands. You could only see the back of our heads but somehow you could tell we were smiling. My palms were sweaty with excitement as I stretched my scrawny arm towards her, the painting clutched in my fingertips. But her eyes showed nothing, not even a flicker. She looked right through the page as though it was just a blank sheet of paper, then she let it float out of her hand and it glided slowly to the floor. Her eyes still stared ahead, as though she'd seen nothing, nothing at all. My eyes were glued to the painting, lying face up on the floor. I bent down quickly and picked it up. Without looking at Eliza, I left the room, something breaking inside me.

After that, I kept my distance. I thought Eliza was a friend, a big sister even, but now, I couldn't look at her without seeing my painting of us holding hands, sliding, forgotten to the ground. She hadn't seen the painting, she hadn't seen me. *How could I rely on her again?* And yet, I did. Gradually, like a fire flickering a little and then taking light, I began to open up to Eliza once more. She was back to herself, back to spinning me round and laughing, back to taking me to the stream and spotting the fishes. Only this time, I kept remembering her blank eyes, unseeing as my painting floated to the floor. Still, I was just a kid then. I was only ten years old and ready to forgive, ready to have my friend back. Now it's not so easy. Now I have to face those blank eyes again, and I'm not sure I can.

The Four Horsemen on the Bus

by Milly Watson

The drizzle had soaked through the flimsy wool of Belinda's coat – worsened by the chill of mid-November, the wind flattening her clothes tighter against her body in a smothering press – meaning it was a surprise against the mundane of Thursday when she turned away from presenting her day return ticket.

Four people sat across the back row of the bus. The usually empty bus, with only its driver and Foughtman Solicitors' longest serving secretary for inhabitants (and even then, they were ghosts loitering about the seats).

Bikers, Belinda realised as she made her way to her usual seat – positioned just in front of the quartet, up against the corner where she could sink down with some illusion of privacy and play her shift's events round in her head (never missing a cringe at some mistake she'd made).

They wore riding leathers in a strange combination of colours – black, red, green and dark grey – each presenting a different state of quality and embellishment. Black was sleek and crisply pressed of creases, comfortably emphasising the wearer's gaunt physique; red decorated in golden accents, glimmering with the indent of medals and the scales of battle armour; green's faded and peeling slightly around the edges, with old smears of oil running along the sleeves; dark grey neat and heavy, the most simplistic design, built for practicality.

A sweat broke out on her palms.

At fifty-two, Belinda didn't consider herself a particularly judgmental woman. Yes, she often struggled to keep up with the news her niece was hurling back from university (the only grandchild her mother had been given thanks to Jeanie and her disastrous try at marriage, which lasted all of five minutes), but she couldn't deny the clench in her gut as intimidation set in.

Unfamiliarity and change in routines was never something she had particularly handled well, yet the presence of four unknown people to the norm was a bit much. Especially after yet another gruelling day listening to the latest saga in *Jodie and Michael's Tumultuous Love Story* – weekly instalments bringing only the urge to permanently glue her forehead to her desk. But now, that same old discord felt positively comforting.

'No!' A small voice sounded in Belinda's head, fingers curling into clenched fists as her eyes settled on her usual seat. *She'd* been the one working yet another monotonous shift – receiving varying degrees of abuse and scorn from clients – only to be met by no real reward upon coming home, aside from maybe a phone call from her niece enquiring about Belinda's life. She was not going to be moved just because some gaggle of road warriors had made themselves present in her sphere of normality.

Sitting down felt like a triumph.

The headiness of satisfaction was so thick about

her, Belinda barely noticed the shortest biker was taking a drag of a cigarette (the smoke a particularly congested plume of black): something entirely illegal on public buses since 2007.

No, instead her attentions were focused on the whirring blur of unloved old corner shops and vandalised bus shelters, as the countryside loomed on the horizon.

"Excuse me?" Belinda couldn't stop herself from turning round, the polite gestures of work well-worn into her bones. It had come from the biker dressed in green – a young man who seemed not a day over twenty-two, with a complexion she could only describe as pasty. "Do you know how many stops it is until we reach the junction to Hixley-Upon-Stratham?"

Before she could reply, the one in red – a woman, not much older than Green, with an explosion of scarlet curls framing a face so sweet it would've caused a scrap between the workmen renovating the office, of that Belinda was certain – cut in.

"Were you even paying attention earlier when we stopped that wanker outside of Sainsbury's?"

Dark Grey made a sound of disapproval, turning in the direction of Red. Their eyes were hidden behind the large helmet, yet Belinda had no doubt a chastising glower was being directed at the girl.

"Look he was an absolute tool!" she protested. "Even you have to admit that, D…"

"Just because he wasn't particularly helpful, it doesn't mean he's earned ridicule." The calmness of the reply was worn not just in the words, but the tone...something about the faceless biker's voice carried finality. She didn't even feel anxious when her reflection came back to meet her, pale eyes wide, the thinness of her face reflected in the visor of Dark Grey's helmet. "It's three stops, isn't it?"

"Yes." Politeness – and a loathing of awkward silences (even if one hadn't been confirmed), caused Belinda to continue. "Hixley-Upon-Stratham, that's quite remote isn't it?"

"We're going to an event," explained Red with a dazzling smile. The harshness of her stare reminded Belinda of the woman who lived at 86, Verity Snodgrass, who glowered at every beaten down postal worker unlucky enough to grace her doorstep and spoke to the receptionist as if she were a particularly naive Year 7. Resentment began to bubble nicely at the back of Belinda's throat. "The North East's Ultimate Bikers Convention."

"One of the largest in the country," explained the Tallest Rider. "Thousands of enthusiasts, newbies and seasoned pros gather for a long weekend spent dedicated to their mutual passion."

Red's eyes were blazing. "And they end up fighting over whose bike's the best."

Smoke billowed from the tip of Green's cigarette. "Spread flu bought from each corner of the United Kingdom, alongside catching norovirus from poorly prepared food."

Black's pearly canine teeth were incredibly sharp when he flashed a grin. "Which clogs their arteries from all the grease and fat it's slathered in."

"But really it's just a nice chance to bond as family

and meet like-minded folk," finished Dark Grey. If Belinda could see their face, she knew a contented smile would be greeting her.

"Oh," she nodded politely. "Well, I hope you all have a lovely time!"

"It's the first time being hosted in such a picturesque little village," the pasty youth seemed disappointed, plucking his cigarette between two fingers wrapped in plasters. "People care so much about appearances there, picking up their litter and hosting whole protests when you so much as think the words 'nuclear power plant'."

Belinda, who had loathed every minute of growing up in Reedness, nodded in sympathy. "Well it can be a bit pedantic I suppose."

Green clicked his fingers. "That's the word!"

"It's all the chemicals he works with," cut in Black with a sharp flash of deep eyes, the teasing tone of an older brother clawing at part of Belinda's heart (Jeanie had always been kind in her frazzled conduct, it was Mum who specialised in mockery). "Makes his concentration terrible."

"Just because you're married to your business!"

"Touché." The eye roll was exaggerated, as if he was savouring the moment. "You may have heard of my company: Simple, Tasty, Affordable, Reliable, Varied and Expansive Incorporated?"

"Yes." Diet foods and a myriad of health supplements, weight loss pills and meal suppressants – all of which were sold at perfectly reasonable prices, to the delight of millions. Yet it was hunger of an entirely different kind that was bubbling in the pit of

Belinda's stomach. "Pardon me for asking, but why aren't you on your bikes?"

"We left them at the event grounds to do some sight-seeing today," Dark Grey told her. "It seemed counterintuitive wasting fuel when we had other means of transport. Plus...some people find our rides a little too exciting."

"Total killjoys." Red was quick to burst into the conversation and voice her displeasure, reverberating off the enclosed vehicle with commanding intensity. "A change to the system can do some good. Chaos brings about much needed upheaval! You see it a *tonne* in my line of work."

Belinda nodded, and couldn't help but agree: wild changes were surprisingly prevalent at a solicitors office (and not just through the lens of clients' behaviour).

Something about that though made an itch begin to rise within the pit of her stomach. The casual dismissal always being thrown at her – be it phone calls with Mum, the entitled people barking orders at her down the phone, her neighbour's constant assumptions she had nothing better to do than come running at their beck and call – how infuriating it was...how it dug beneath her skin and gnawed away at her self-esteem...

But maybe she was just in a bad mood because she was hungry?

Since getting on the bus, her stomach had been steadily getting louder in its grumblings for food, and not the sort Belinda knew she should be having. Slathered in oil and artificial flavourings, dripping with saturated fat and layers of salt, complete junk that would do her figure no favours...but the craving only seemed to intensify by the moment.

"Where are you off to then?" Black's voice cut through her train of thought, smooth as a knife slicing butter, and his eyes were shining with some sort of self-assurance when she met them.

"Oh just home." Truly, Belinda felt a little embarrassed to admit as such. It wasn't every day you met bikers bound for Hixley-Upon-Stratham, yet there she was (pudgy, pasty old Belinda McInday), merely bound to the same routine. Sometimes, she could admit to herself it felt close to a choke hold. "I haven't got much exciting planned really...just calling my mother to make sure she's taken her heart medication and sorting out some books to send to Oxfam."

"There's no shame in that," Dark Grey began to reassure her, but Green had perked up, a puff of smoke oozing from his cigarette as he turned towards her.

"Pills?"

Belinda nodded. "Just beta-blockers...sometimes I feel she doesn't take them just to be difficult. Half the time I talk to her, it's like she just wants to fight for no good reason."

"Maybe give her some space?" the young man suggested – an energy about him which had come from somewhere untraceable. When she'd first gotten onto the bus, he'd seemed lethargic and bordering upon sleep from where he'd been slumped against the window. "Sometimes, I find people can benefit from just taking a step back and letting nature take its due cour…"

Dark Grey cleared their throat sharply then, head turned towards Green, hidden eyes undeniable in where their glower was being directed. An older sibling correcting the younger, no doubt.

"What?" A pasty brow furrowed as the boy's lips formed into a pout.

"Please excuse him." The Tallest Rider's voice was apologetic as they turned back to Belinda. "He went through quite a rough patch and it's left him a little overzealous to give advice, even when the timing is inappropriate."

"Oh no, it's fine!" She was loath to leave their conversation on an awkward note. Glancing out the window, she recognised the gaudy sign of The Guitar and Staff from where it stuck out just past the brow beaten sign signalling they had now officially entered Guildington. Home was just on the horizon, so far away from the excitement of a biker rally, mundane and comforting yes – but sometimes, Belinda could admit to herself that there was a twinge of boredom that came alongside the terracotta brick work and lazily tended flower beds.

Resentment lurched into the back of her throat and she did her best to swallow it back down.

"I take it we're almost at your stop?" Dark Grey enquired, hands placed in their lap...the gloves were large, yes, but the digits beneath them seemed so thin when Belinda caught a glance. Like matchsticks in their thinness...almost skeletal. In a slight daze – a long day and stomach grumbling furiously – she nodded. "Well it's been a pleasure meeting you."

She blinked quickly as she glanced at all four of them. In the reflection of the Tallest Rider's visor, the same round cheeks and loose strays of soft brown hair greeted her, yet something new was bubbling away, Belinda could feel it (either that or two cheese and pickle sandwiches with a cuppa really weren't enough for lunch).

"Likewise," the nod was more for own reassurance, but none of them made to mock her nervous habit. "I hope that your event goes well."

"Oh we're certain it will!" Red announced, leaning forward so quickly for a moment Belinda thought she was about to launch out of her seat. "It'll be a total riot!"

"Figuratively or literally?" Black shot the shorter biker a sly look.

"Either's good."

Belinda pressed the bell, glancing once more out to the row of houses split by the post office, and then back at the fellow passengers she was leaving behind. A pale, sickly flame was rising from Green's lighter, breathing life into another cigarette as tarrish smoke curled from the corners of his mouth. Black, Red, and Dark Grey were merely still.

The bus lurched to a halt, but Belinda knew better than prematurely trying to get out of her seat.

"Well it was lovely meeting you all," she said. "I don't suppose I'll see you again, so best of wishes for your convention."

Red gave her a salute, Black a polite nod, Green's plastered thumb turned upwards. The Tallest Rider merely tilted their head up slightly.

"I will see you again Belinda," the voice was calm...an assurance, a promise. "But not for some time. So, all I can wish is that life treats you better until then."

"Oh, um, til' next time." She cringed at the briskness of her wave, yet if any of the four found this amusing (or, more likely than not, pitiable), nothing showed.

Stepping into the cool air, Belinda blinked quickly to adjust her eyes to the filter of rain – a little calmer in its descent from the heavens, but still persistent. Her stomach was clenching with something indescribable though.

She was finally going to give Mum a piece of her mind about all those years of unfair comparison, celebrate with a bottle of prosecco and the greasiest pizza she could get her hands on, say sod it to all the unfair expectations of the world – her thoughts were cut off by a sneeze. Dammit, the rain had given her a cold it seemed. Well, all of that could come after she'd had a lemsip.

This is Where the Magic Happens

By Helen Kenwright

It's not the words that are the problem
It's the images in my head
That won't make it out
It's not the ideas that are the problem
It's the words that somehow
Don't coalesce on the page
Instead they
Coagulate
In the brain
Like cold barley stew

There's not enough time
There's too much time
There's never the right time
To write

I'm here to tell you
You have the time
You have the ideas
You have the words

Take up your pen
Your prompt is freedom
Ten minutes.
Starting now:
Write.

Magic.

The Diaries of Pandemic Objects
by Abbie-Rose Reddington

Hand Sanitiser 12.4.2020

Casually, I sit here. On the sideboard. It gets quite lonely. No friends to talk to, I occasionally see small versions of myself get pulled out of my owners' bag, but they do not tend to be very friendly. They just brag about the adventures they get to go on. I do wonder why I do not get to go on these adventures. They say it is because I am not small enough to fit into their bags! I thought having extra supply in me was a good thing! I get attention but not enough to satisfy me and I get barely glanced at even when I do dispense cleanliness to these bacteria ridden people. However, recently they have been coming to me more and more and I cannot understand what I am doing differently to get so much attention!

I suppose I should tell you about my owners. The main one is Bluey, she is alright I suppose. She gives me the most attention. The second is Beans. She gives me less attention. She rants when Bluey gives me attention. Beans says how the more Bluey utilizes me the less of an effect it will have on her. I do not quite understand this myself. I think Beans is just jealous of my receiving of Bluey's recognition.

Face Mask 18.8.2020

Hi, I sit on people's faces. I appear to be very controversial in the outside world for some reason at the moment on whether I am effective or not. I am not used to this. Everyone is wearing me! I am not sure I quite like it! I am used to people only wearing me in very specific scenarios such as medical situations. The outside world is quite scary! Though I do keep spotting humans wearing me under their noses. This confuses me a lot. Why wear me if you do not do it properly? When we get home I get chucked down next to this hand sanitiser guy who thinks he is the best and everyone should love him. I really do not like him at all! I would much rather be clung on to the lanyard than dumped next to him…

Hand Sanitiser 20.9.2020

I finally found out why people are paying me more attention. I overheard a conversation. It is to do with this pandemic currently happening, whoever that is? But I like this pandemic being, they have finally made people understand why I am so loveable! I am friends with them already! I wonder how I can meet them. Maybe they are like a god?

Poppy Lanyard 6.10.2020

I am the one who everyone wants to cling on to. I am unsure why, but it is great fun! I am just glad I do not have to have Mr "I'm so great" attached to me. I suppose you want a description of me. Well, I am green and have yellow sunflowers printed all over me. I seem to recall Bluey telling Beans that I am to inform people that she has a hidden disability and may need extra support as she is blind. I feel powerful with this role! Though, I am not sure why silly society cannot work it out for themselves since she uses a white cane! Me and the cane are a dream team! We all are really except for that big bottle of hand sanitiser.

Covid 24.11.2020

I just do not like humans. Yuck! They try to get rid of me with hand sanitiser and they try and hide from me behind face masks and inside their houses. See, I can control them even though they cannot even see me. I have power!

Hand Sanitiser 4.1.2021

I cannot believe the stupid face mask got to go out with Bluey AGAIN. I am so much more clever killing bacteria than just being a piece of cloth over their mouth stopping them from breathing. All I want is an adventure. The face mask always seems to come home with gossip. I have to act friendly just to get it though. I am unsure if he gives me it all.

"Hey, you want to give me some gossip then bud?"

"Bud? I am not your bud…I hate you!"

"Come on. We live together. We have to get on."

"OK fine! They are thinking of another

lockdown."

"Lockdown? What's that?"

"Oh come on! Catch up! It is where everyone has to stay at home. Everything is shut."

Face Mask 22.5.2021

WHY HAVE I BEEN THROWN DOWN NEXT TO THE HAND SANITISER? I HAVE ONLY JUST BEEN WASHED! I really do not want to be here next to this loud mouth acting as if we are 'buds'. He talks to me as if he is superior and is clearly jealous of how I get to go on adventures.

"Where did you get to go today then?" he said in a snooty voice.

"Oh it was great we went to the pub! I even got a bit of gin spilt on me. It was very tasty!"

"I bet Bluey will take me instead of you next time."

"Why would she do that? She has a mini you who is much more convenient."

Covid 23.5.2021

The people seem to be winning…I am losing my power! I found out they have had this vaccine going around a few months now to try and prevent me infecting them! I cannot let them win, I cannot let them take power over me! I am losing hope and they are gaining it. This was not my plan!

A Legacy of Celestials and Amphibians

by Llykaell Dert-Ethrae

A tickle of trees wander all about
Stroking with limbs and giving a shout
To all those napkins and singing trout
That dinner is ready, beyond any doubt.

I've nothing to say as the matter is closed
I'm sorry I've done nothing, through all I've dosed
Through all these tomes I've eyed and nosed
My teacup is sad, overall it's morose.

Sea shanty wine cups putter o'er head
And penguins chatter so noisily in their stead,
With great gusto the chorus meanders a thread
And is so terrible that we all ended up dead.

Cries and malarkies, dances and chirps
The fire is dying, the drunks and their derps,
A burning of toes follow a hosting of burps
Parading chandeliers and singing like twerps.

The angle of incidence is the angle of rhyme
Her legs are splayed, spread open through time.
A rambunctious descent to moan out a chime
Lubricious intent, a dance turns on a dime.

Triangular eagles profess with a screech
That we're all invited to have fun at the beach.
The tingling lube is just out of reach
For the wise eel has one more lesson to teach.

It slithers about, seeing all with keen eyes
Craving and lusting after key lime pies
Snorting cocaine, it severs all ties
With the world and all the pastries of lies.

So here we all are at the edge of the gate
Brooding in our garden that's just growing slate
A peacock wanders in with an arrogant gait
To tell all our fortunes, our destined fate.

Swilling a shot, it shuffles its feet
And ruffles its feathers until they are neat
It opens its beak preparing to greet
But is silenced by a torrent of sleet!

Porcupine eyes glower in from behind
Gnawing at the leftover smelly cheese rind
They take to the stage and blow the mind
Of the dead bird and all else they could find.

The intrepid tea-cosy with its warm quilt,
Sticks its nose in without any guilt
Poking round the door, it spies with a tilt
And learns all about what the space frogs have built!

Glowing angels in their library of hush

Sit with lions they keep urging to shush
They grind up peas and turn them to mush
That taste so divine we cannot help but gush.

Bounding in from the cold with their strong legs
The amphibians drink everything down to the dregs
They sing with drunk angels who demand further kegs
Until bar-pirates concede, hobbling in on their pegs.

Yellow stone tablets with chalks of hot pink
Tell the great tales of a ship that could sink
To build it with holes so air could it drink
"For better floatation", or so they did think…

The nebula fish with its eyes open wide
Looks down on it all with remarks that deride
Sneering at the cavorts at each solar tide
The space frogs do laugh as it turns aside.

Standing over the dead bird's epitaph
Is a most inquisitive top-hatted giraffe.
It gives it a sniff and makes ticks on a graph
And says, "Well now, that separates the wheat from the chaff!"

As the music picks up, all present do jive
With the exception of few, who break out in a hive
From the orbiting board into the sea they all dive
Then thank life-guard eagles who keep them alive.

The solar seas yield just for the brave

And the tales of all others are nothing if not grave
Yet angels and frogs, unsure of how to behave,
Leap blindly right into the nearest star wave!

The authors and tellers of that story knew nowt,
For all parties were fine as they swam all about
Perhaps they were made of stern stuff and of stout,
But such a mess did they leave – oh my all that grout!

The bar-pirates incensed, they summoned their dean
Who looked on in horror at all they must clean
The stench was enough to make the brigands turn green
Like the frogs and their cohorts who had been so mean.

And so angels and frogs were forced to look hard
At the nebula pool they so badly had marred
The pirates all glowered and gave them a card
To the cupboard and told them to clean the whole yard.

Yet in their haste to make the stars newly shine
They had used too much force, making them all realign!
The heavens mixed up, the pirates were lost in the brine
Leaving frogs and angels alone to party and dine!

Mindful Guidance

By Christina O'Reilly

I trip and am caught by a big pair of hands
I stumble and tumble and again I am saved
by this big pair of hands
I can't see, can see, won't see, don't see
And still those hands gather me up and
slowly guide me
Who after many times and things that have
happened
Filter through the scare, share, joy, pain,
happy, sad, mad and bad
Who pull their fingers through the darkness,
lightness of my mind
Like a mother gently running her fingers
through my hair
Whose hands are these?
Always there ready to lift, carry, push, drive,
and hold me
They are my mind's hands
Guiding me back to safety

Some Things Never Change

by Junior Mark Cryle

On a Spaceport orbiting the planet, stands the CAPTAIN on the Bridge, enjoying a mug of tea.

Enter OFFICER FLANNIGAN.

F: Captain, I have the latest report.

C: Perfect timing. **(sip)** What's on our schedule today, Miss Flannigan?

F: The representatives from Galaxies 101-104 are due to arrive at the agreed meeting times, Captain. Galaxies 106-109 have confirmed their attendance for tomorrow's conference, and Galaxy 105 have messaged an apology as they've encountered heavy traffic.

C: Duly noted, Officer. **(sip)** Anything else?

F: There's a backlog of applications for alien representatives, in hopes to have their say in interstellar matters. Most frequent of which being from the "Vampires of Saturns".

C; They need to be processed in Offworld Affairs, which is not our department. **(beat)** Wait, run that one by me again?

F: The Vampires of Saturn, Captain.

C: As in 'Creatures of the night,' on a gaseous windy planet, with no solid footing at all?

F: They're currently stationed on Earth, Captain.

C: Furthermore, Vampires in space. As in, "Bram Stoker's Dracula" Vampires? In Space?

F: Actually, their Bio-Scans confirmed them to be Homosapiens. Live Homosapiens.

C: But why Vampires?

F: They felt the Undead were misrepresented, and therefore hoped to acquire respect by being identified as an independent species.

C: Well **(sip)**, at least they're the only ones to-

F: They're not the only ones.

C: Of course not!

F: They include: The Asteroid Farmers of Mars.

AKA: Vegan students of Princeton University, USA, Homosapiens…

C: **(muttered)** Knew I was an Oxford man for some reason.

F: … The Beastfolk of Pluto. AKA: A gang of hairy bikers, also Homosapiens…

C: **(muttered)** Can't believe we assumed it was a real planet.

F: … and the Velocity Valkyries of Venus. AKA-

C: Let me guess: the Housewives of Manchester United Football Club's Catering Department, who are, and I'm spitballing here, Homosapiens?

F: **(beat)** So you've read the report, Captain?

C: And these are among how many applicants?

F: One-third of Earth's Populous, which estimates to be 2.34 Billion.

C: Good grief. **(gulps mouthful of tea)** Dare I ask why?

F: The sentiment that Extraterrestrials, or E.Ts, are misrepresented and refuse to be associated with a race of "insensitive Poopy-Heads", is the first most frequent of reasons.

C: Of course, not like we're seen as alien to EVERYONE ELSE in the universe.

(gulps more tea) At least it can't get worse than-

F: It gets worse, Captain.

C: **(sighs)** Please elaborate.

F: Among those applicants, two-thirds of them have also made petitions to form their own off-world colonies. The primary reason, among countless more, being: "I refuse to live on a planet without any respect" or, at least, it's our best translation given their 'unique' choice of words.

C: To get away from people treating you differently based on your looks and behaviour? What an excellent use of a system that was designed for the sole purpose of enabling Earthlings to live on other worlds within suitable artificial environments. Why didn't WE think of that before?

F: **(beat)** Captain, are you being sarcasti-

C: OF COURSE I'M BEING SARCASTIC! It's stupid, That's what it is. For every person who's "practically perfect in every way" there's fifty more forming their own movements. Undead First, E.T.W.s, Fertalism, Anti E.T.W.s, Anti-Fertalism, Anti Anti E.T.W.s, even the I.M.Ts.

F: "Interspecies, Mindmelding, and Transdimensional"? How is that relevant?

C: They're all "Schrodinger's Topics", both irrelevant and relevant until someone points them out and it becomes the ONE SUBJECT that supersedes everything else. EVERYTHING! Then there's those who think they are the reincarnated spirits of trees, or believe they deserve the same rewards as everyone else with no regards to how the economic system works, or even those who claim to be targets of discrimination when literally five minutes prior they just targeted other beings for the EXACT, SAME, REASONS! GAAAHHHHHH!!!!!! **(deep breath x3)** It's official, I'm on the Planet of Hypocrisy. **(sips)**

F: To be fair, Captain, these were just from the top of the pile. With time, there's a guarantee that there'll be requests with genuine justifications to be found, but are buried underneath this mess, and will stay buried if we give up on them.

C: **(sigh)** True enough. And I suppose judging the whole by the acts of the few doesn't help matters in the long run, yet ironically it only takes a few to change the course towards the future. In the end, we can only control ourselves and I, for one, intend to keep my mind open and listen to what needs to be heard, for better or worse.

F: I wholeheartedly agree, Captain.

C: **(sips)** I still think everyone's a hypocrite.

F: I wholeheartedly agree, Captain. **(pause)** May I ask a personal question?

C; Proceed. **(sip)**

F: How many Mugs of Tea have you had this morning, Captain?

C: Still on my first. **(clatter of knocked empty mugs was heard, as he sips)** Batch.

F: A Baker's Dozen again?

C: No. **(more clatter, another sip)** A Baker's Dozen's Dozen.

F: Maybe you should stop, Captain. Dr. Hoozear did advise you on your Tea related problems and-

C: I can stop whenever I want, too much tea never kills anyone, and what doesn't kill you makes you stronger. **(finishes tea then adds mug to the pile)** In which case, **(opens communication)** Lottie, One Mug of Tea. Triple Strength.

F: Triple? But your bowels, Captain, they cannot take the strain.

C; I know what I can handle, Miss Flannigan, thank you. Beam it up, Lottie.

A new Mug of Tea appears in CAPTAIN's hand. CAPTAIN sips. Pause.

C: I immediately regret my decision. **(runs off)** GANG WAY!

END

The Nature of Flame

By Ross

She was blunt; that's the first thing that popped into his mind about meeting her. She was crude, bold and blunt. What kind of woman gets mad at a man for getting in the way of her thrown boulder? And the casual proposition for after her training… he was getting flushed just recalling it! Still, he was eager to study pyromancy, and she was the one to go to, so he resolved to endure her crass remarks and demeanour to gain a tutor.

He couldn't go into this half-heartedly; she wouldn't let him. He had to live with her, hunt and eat with her and get up before the first rays of dawn to train. Getting up late resulted in his head getting dunked in water, if he was lucky.

The noble ladies he was used to all knew which fork to use for each dish and took dainty mouthfuls. This woman took a handful of leg and tore meat from bone savagely with her incisors and canines before wolfing it down. The noble ladies he was used to could name the most famous artists and describe their techniques. This woman called all art "prissy bull" and said they should all do "real work".

"So, Beansprout, why'd you come to me for this in the first place?" Hilde asked. Roy had hoped that her nickname for him would wear off at some point during this training, but it seemed that "Roy Renaistelle" was a name she could not, or would not, remember.

Roy swallowed his bite of mutton before replying. "I aspire to become a tactician of Greenveil. While I am no doubt going to have my own bodyguards," *for my military position instead of nobility, for a change,* "all tacticians are officially required to be proficient in one arcane and one mundane martial art." He spotted another tear in the cotton of his tunic, but at least there were no new stains. *This woman will be the death of me.* "I know it seems superfluous, but the red tape is there."

Hilde smirked. "Ha! For a few seconds there, I almost had some respect for you! Superfluous!"

"What? It's true!"

"The closer you are to your soldiers, the faster and more reliably you can issue them orders. Soldiers tend to be on the battlefield, you know? Surveying the area of engagement is easier in person too. If you can't see why it's good to have combat skills when personally on the battlefield, you might as well have spent your precious tactical education scratching your ass."

"You... you are... just shut up and be grateful the people of Greenveil chose to pay you for your services! You are insufferable!"

"You think the money is why I'm doing this? They're paying me a pittance, genius." Hilde raised her hand towards Roy, slowly raising her fingers. It looked like she was flipping him off until she raised a third finger. "This much gold, in as many months." She let out a snort.

Roy was speechless. His own personal spending budget was triple that for the fortnight. An uneasy silence reigned for half a minute.

Roy found his voice again to ask the only question he could possibly ask in response to that. "Why? Why did you agree to teach me?"

Hilde regained that same smirk on her face. "Prove to me that your education wasn't a total waste. Figure it out for yourself, Beansprout."

On that note, she left him to ponder. *Figure it out myself, eh?* Roy refused to back down from a mental challenge.

Tansy

by William Davidson

Tom edged away from the crowd at Rachel and Rick's house-warming party. He walked to the end of the garden that backed onto the Ouse. Tansy plants lined the riverbank, their small yellow flowers shining in the sunlight.

'We're going to clear all this, Tommy lad.' Rick was striding towards him and taking puffs of his cigar.

Tom had tried his best with Rick over the years, but he still couldn't understand what Rachel saw in him. But Tom felt a duty to make an effort. You had to with in-laws – they were always going to be around.

'We'll dig out these weeds and put in a landing,' said Rick. 'A sort of jetty. We're going to get a boat.'

Rick nodded to himself behind a cloud of cigar smoke.

'Tansy plants aren't any old weed,' said Tom.

'There's a lovely cruiser I've got my eye on,' said Rick. 'Thirty-eight foot. Six berths. Teak decking. Acrylic awning. Diesel, of course.'

'Of course,' said Tom. 'You see, tansy plants are home to tansy beetles. Tansy beetles only live on tansy plants, and only in York.'

'Silent flush toilet,' said Rick. 'Electric bilge pump.'

Rick was gesticulating at the river as if he were trying to summon up his dream boat.

'So you can't just dig them up,' said Tom. 'They're rare.'

'What are?' said Rick.

'Tansy beetles.'

'Tansy pansy. I won't tell if you don't. It'll be worth it. You won't be whinging about your creepy crawlies when we take you for a nice trip downriver. You and me in the cockpit. Gins in hand. Just picture it, Tommy.'

Tom tried hard not to picture it.

'We might find a few now,' said Tom. He knelt by one of the plants and started turning over its leaves.

'Alright, Chris Packham,' said Rick. 'Tenner says I'll find one first.'

Even an encounter with wildlife had to have a monetary incentive for Rick. Tom watched him throw his cigar into the river like he was practising his darts, and then crouch by a tansy plant a few feet away. Rick examined the leaves like he was reading the small print on a contract. They were silent for a while.

'Oh,' said Rick. 'Oh right.'

'Have you found one?' said Tom.

'Oh,' said Rick. 'You didn't say they were…'

Rick seemed to be mesmerised, gazing close at the tansy beetle.

'Beautiful?' said Tom. 'Jewel-like?'

When Rick looked at Tom, his eyes were moist and glinting.

'Yeah,' said Rick. 'My old nan had a brooch like this fella. She wore it every day, like it was a sort of talisman. She said it was precious. That's the word she used. She said you've always got to recognise what's precious.'

Rick turned the leaf over again and sat back on the grass.

'Oh,' he said, and then he didn't talk for a long time but just watched the tansy plants and the water beyond them, and not a single boat passed by.

The Miracle of Our Hands

by Charley Perryn

Whilst being part of Converge at the Haven Creative Spaces class, I took part in a three week in depth look at the subject of our hands. It made me realise how amazing our hands are and how much I take them for granted. This poem reflects the insights I gained from listening to everybody's contributions and my own realizations.

Attached to our arms,
Our hands are
The eyes of the heart.
As we touch and feel
And connect to our world.

Our fingerprints are unique to us.
We are all different, yet
Our hands connect us to
Each other,
Our hands help us
Feel what it is to be human.

For through touch, love

Is made tangible, into
A concept we can understand.
Without words
The language of the heart,
Is expressed through the holding of hands,
Or a warm embrace.
To bring comfort and reassurance
To feel togetherness,
To protect from harm,
To wave hello!
To say goodbye,
To sign and communicate,
To perceive the world through our fingertips,
If our eyes no longer have sight.

Our hands can create magic!
Craft beautiful creations,
Sculpt amazing objects,
Paint our own masterpieces.
Write beautiful poetry!

We can hold hands and stand in solidarity,
To fight for a more compassionate world.
Where hands are used to create peace
And no longer carry weapons of war.

And the memory of touch…
Of our loved ones who have passed away.
Lives on within us.
For love can never die, it is an eternal
Bond, imprinted upon the heart for ever
And our hands gave us that gift,

To feel that soul connection,
To hold the heart of another
In our hands, perhaps the greatest
Gift of all.

And in a covid world,
Where the holding of hands and hugging
Is strictly forbidden,
Unless it's a hand that lives
In your household,
Souls have become lonely
As somehow Zoom fatigue
Sets in and a screen is no
Replacement for human touch.

Hands can harm
And break a heart,
But hands can soothe
And heal a heart!

The miracle of our hands.

About Our Authors

Abbie-Rose is an Occupational Therapy student. She originates from south of England but studies in the North. Abbie has a strong sense of humour which she demonstrates through her creative writing. Abbie has reflected on the last year of all our lives and has written her piece based on this.

Caroline lives in Yorkshire, her adopted home. She is still developing her writing style but definitely likes adding a bit of humour.
This years story has been inspired by her friends The Gordons. She just hopes they still talk to her once they see themselves immortalised and caricatured in print!

Catherine was born and brought up in the countryside, but left to go to the city to
become a university student. Her latest hobby is learning to play the ukulele with Converge.
She would like to thank the Converge tutors and support staff for being cheerful and keeping everyone going during lockdown.

Charley lives in North Yorkshire with her dog Harry. She is an abstract artist and poet. The art she creates is inspired by the poetry she writes and vice versa. Charley finds inspiration for her creativity on her walks with Harry in nature, at York Art Gallery and through Converge Classes.
Charley also loves lego and continues to build her lego

model railway!

Christina lives outside of York with her husband Paul. Christina got her ideas from the extra curriculum class in January called "Art to Inspire". One was on "Serialism" her piece called Mindful Guidance came from a thought after class that turned into her poem.
A class on "Impressionists" paintings – one of which was painted by Gustave Caillebotte called "Woman at the Window" painted in 1880 inspired Christina to write her story Charlotte. Long live the escapism of Creative Writing.

Esther Clare Griffiths is a songwriter, mum and writer (not necessarily in that order!) She loves to write with her dog, Jackson, snuggled up next to her – he's a great audience and never quick to judge! In her memoirs, Esther writes of growing up in Northern Ireland - firm friends, a tin tub bath by the fire and long walks in search of wine gums! She loves her work for Converge & Emerging Voices as songwriting tutor and co-leader of Communitas choir, and is working with her students to record their original songs. Esther released a new album earlier this year, 'Beneath Our Dreams' - do have a listen for free! www.estherclare.bandcamp.com

Helen Kenwright writes speculative fiction and romance novels and short stories, and occasionally resorts to poetry. There's usually dragons. She lives in

York with two cats, one of whom is now employed as a part time classroom assistant on Zoom.

Holly: Punctuation disliker. Occasional poem writer.

Junior Mark Cryle was born and raised in the City of York, and lives with creativity as a self-certified dragon fanatic, from a love of illustrations to an interest in mythology. An optimist when it comes to fiction and life, he reflects this trait in his work as he takes pride in giving enjoyment to those around him. A silver tongue in conversation and a black belt in Karate, he is a force to be reckoned with.

Karen is an Alien Spy who disguises herself as a human being when she visits Earth. Her favourite way to spend her free time is to hang out with her earthling friends and family, but she does sometimes like to go back to her own planet for some peace and quiet.

Keith lives in North Yorkshire. He has done creative writing for a number of years. Some of it has been put into books for people to enjoy. He is classed as a mature student.

Kevin Keld currently resides within the beautiful Yorkshire Wolds after returning from a ten year spell in the mountains of Southern Spain in 2015. The recent pandemic has allowed him to finally complete his first book The Motorcycle Undertaker detailing his thirty years in the business of buying, selling and dismantling motorcycles. He wrote countless articles for several motorcycle related magazines in the late nineties and even had his own column in one dealing with technical issues. Humour features very heavily in both the articles and the recent book and another book is almost complete chronicling a year in the life of a pet Dalek that took up residence in the church house in Spain. At present, the author is recovering from a serious motorcycle accident using the free time to write even more two-wheeled tales of bravery and derring-do.

Lucy grew up in Essex and Cheshire but has called York her home since 2004. She graduated with a degree in Education and IT from York St John University in 2008 and chose to continue living in the city. Lucy lives with her cheeky, elderly house rabbit Jasper who rules the roost and thinks he is the boss. In her spare time Lucy is an avid reader and also enjoys a variety of crafts and blog writing.

Llykaell Dert-Ethrae was born in the suburbs of Aldvon on Covyn 5. She is currently one of the most prolific publishers on Ancient History for the Covyn Historical Society (CHS) and holds one of the chairs on their Board. Her best friend is renowned Project C, the only person in Covyn to publish more books on Ancient History than Lykaell. She currently resides in Lios where the headquarters of the CHS sits. Lykaell spends her free time running around like a little girl hugging trees and chasing cats as well as going off to exotic archaeological expeditions with her friend

Project C.

Llykaell's first book, *The Immortals of Covyn: Part 1* was published in 2021, and is available from Amazon. https://www.amazon.co.uk/dp/B09M6S8T1M

Mary: A biopic of Mary Catherine Palmer

Born in the City, Of Birmingham,
At 10 we moved house to the countryside.
From the bleak, street lined terraced houses.
To cows grazing in lush pastures green
Majestic trees with rustled breeze leaves
Flower beds overflowing with pinks & blues
Leapfrogging down the long green lawn.
I loved reading & writing poems, songs & rhymes
Visiting our library & choosing books
But the eldest of six & lots to do.
At 37 I made my home in York
My art still out of reach
In my 67th year with more free time
And YSJ Converge supporting me
I sang and recorded at Abbey Rd Studio
Where The Beatles sang, no less.
I sang Christmas Carols in York Minster
With Communitas Choir & Chris.
I had my painting accepted at
The Ferrens in Hull
I'm growing & knowing in leaps & bounds
Enjoying the new me I have found
Thanks Converge for being around.

Michael Fairclough was last seen around York and is thought to be alarmed and preposterous. He did at one point have chickens as pets and has still not paid the ransom to get them back. Michael can frequently be found waist deep in a pair of trousers or with a good book snuggled up by a fireman. Michael spends his spare time painting, drawing and sculpting when he can get peace and quiet. Michael's work has been described as bizarre and funny, sometimes a bit gruesome, often poignant and almost always surprising. The same could be said about his appearance.

Milly lives in Yorkshire. She enjoys so-bad-it's-good media, thrifting through charity shops, and dreams of the day she can get a pet cat (instead of vicariously living through bonding with other people's). Her creative license had to be exchanged for something and that turned out to be height, so for now she's looking for the perfect stepladder.

Minnie lives in York with her husband and their two dogs. Her work has been published in several charity poetry collections. Minnie enjoys writing science fiction and fantasy but willingly embraces new challenges to broaden her creative abilities. She believes words hold the power to shape the world.

Ross is an amateur author who made his debut with Creative Writing Heals Volume Two. His hobbies include reading, gaming and writing.

Stuart is the author of four books on sewing and quilting and is also a monthly columnist for four of the UKs best loved craft and lifestyle magazines. He is also a popular designer of quiting and dressmaking fabrics and handknitting yarns and his textiles are available worldwide. He is a regular expert judge on Channel 4's "Kirstie's Handmade Christmas" TV show and judges British Dressmaker of the Year alongside a panel of experts from film and theatre. His first love is sewing and writing began as an offshoot of that, creating patterns for shops and magazines in the early 2000s. He switched careers completely in 2011 and has been writing professionally ever since.

Away from work, Stuart and his husband Charles are renovating their families' 90 acre farm in North Yorkshire where they keep a herd of Boer goats, a flock of Welsh Mountain sheep and chickens too naughty to count. He is working on his first novel, of which these two chapters are a part.

TNX Some creative writing.

Zofia grew up in Warwickshire and after visiting her sister, a student at York University, she fell in love with the city and made it her home. Zofia is currently writing her debut novel *A Physical Presence*.

Acknowledgements

Thank you to all our contributors, for having the courage to share their fantastic work.

Thank you to Converge Art Tutor Sylkie de Waard for the amazing cover image.

Thank you to all the Converge students, mentors, supporters and YSJ students for their help.

Thank you to all the staff at Converge for all they've done to support this production.

Thank you to the Igen Trust for resourcing and encouraging us.

And finally, thanks to our production team of Helen, Andy, Clare and William for being a magnificent crew for this year's delayed but victorious voyage of the Great Ship Overly Ambitious!

About Converge

Converge is a partnership between York St John University and mental health service providers in the York region. It offers high quality educational opportunities to those who use NHS and non-statutory mental health services and who are 18 years and over.

Converge was established in 2008 from a simple idea: to offer good quality courses in a university setting to local people who use mental health services taught by students and staff. The development of Converge has progressively demonstrated the potential of offering educational opportunities to people who use mental health services, delivered by students and staff and held on a university campus. This has become the key principle which, today, remains at the heart of Converge. Born of a unique collaboration between the NHS and York St John University, Converge continues to deliver educational opportunities for people with mental health problems.

We offer work-based experience to university students involved in the programme. All classes are taught by undergraduate and postgraduate students, staff and, increasingly people who have lived experience of mental ill health. We have developed a solid track record of delivering quality courses. Careful support and mentoring underpin our work, thereby allowing students to experiment with their own ideas and creativity whilst gaining real world experience in the community. This undoubtedly enhances their employability in an increasingly competitive market.

As a leader in the field, Converge develops symbiotic projects and partnerships which are driven by innovation and best practice. The result is twofold: a rich and exciting educational opportunity for people with mental health problems alongside authentic and practical work experience for university students.

The aims of Converge are to:

- Work together as artists and students
- Build a community where we learn from each other
- Engage and enhance the university and wider community
- Provide a supportive and inclusive environment
- Respect others and value ourselves
- Above all, strive to be ordinary, extraordinary yet ourselves

About the Writing Tree

The Writing Tree is dedicated to the support and nurturing of creative writers. Founded in 2011, the Writing Tree offers tuition, coaching and editing services and publishes work by community groups and other new writers.

The guiding principles of the Writing Tree are that creative writing has importance independent of subject, purpose or audience, and that everyone has the right to write, and to write what they wish.

The Writing Tree is honoured to publish 'Creative Writing Heals' for Converge. All proceeds from the book are donated to further the efforts of Converge writers.

You can find out more about the Writing Tree at www.writingtree.co.uk.

Printed in Great Britain
by Amazon